A DANNY CAVANAUGH MYSTERY

A DANNY CAVANAUGH MYSTERY

Gary Hardwick

HardBooks
Publishing

GRIND CITY Copyright 2016© Gary Hardwick
All rights reserved

ISBN-10 0-9854759-4-3   ISBN-13 978-0-9854759-4-9
HardBooks Publishing
www.garyhardwick.com

First Edition
Cover Design: Gary Hardwick

PUBLISHER'S NOTE

PRAISE FOR CITYCIDE & GARY HARDWICK

"Citycide is the latest, explosively charged murder mystery featuring gritty, street-smart cop Danny Cavanaugh - a white man who grew up amid Detroit's primarily black underclass. The entire city hangs in the balance as Danny races against time, in this exciting, action-packed saga of murder, mayhem, and brutal struggles for power!" Highly recommended.

- Midwest Book Review

"[*Dark Town Redemption*] is a ferocious novel that makes so many other, similar takes on the era read like tame exercises in word spinning."

- Booklist

"There never was and never will be again a hero quite like Danny Cavanaugh."

- Mystery Times Review

"In [*Color Of Justice*] Hardwick presents an unflinching picture... this is thought-provoking crime fiction.

- Library Journal

To my maternal grandmother,
Mozel Tyler.
taken from the water

Author's Note

I knew this day would come.

Many years ago, I created a character named Danny Cavanaugh. He was supposed to die, a sacrifice to the noble character of the reader. But he didn't. Like any real hero, he survived the god-like wrath of the writer and lived on— four books and counting.

Mr. Cavanaugh is a very hard case, the kind of guy you hate to see coming because he cannot lie and can back up all of his truth with facts, fists or bullets, whichever you prefer. And so when he wanted to tell this story himself, how could I say no?

I resisted at first because if he does all the talking, what's my job going to be? I'm a control freak when it comes to my creations and I certainly didn't want this guy running around in my head unbridled.

But of course it would give us all a chance to find out some things about Danny that we've all been wanting to know, you know, personal stuff that only he could talk about.

So, I relented and let him write this one. I knew it would be kind of a wild ride but I also knew that Danny would not bore you.

I can't wait to hear what he has to say.

gch (2015)

Who will protect the public
when the police violate the law?

- Ramsey Clark, Esq.
Former U.S. Attorney General

"There was a while when I was feeling
like, 'Damn, if I'd just been born black, I
would not have to go through all this.'"

- Eminem

"Do we struggle against our goodness or our
evil? The answer to this question is the reason
for our unwavering commitment to murder."

- Joe Black

PROLOGUE

BELLIGERENT

This story begins with violence. It's not on purpose. It's just how people are and not just in Detroit, but everywhere. Don't know why everybody can't see that everything we do is connected to struggle in some way. Even as we seek to love, care and nurture, we keep doing it the hard way. It's our nature, I guess like they keep saying on *Star Trek*.

I'll get to that part later, but first I want you to see some of the good that happens in my city each day, you know, the stuff the media always seems to forget about or else they tack it on the end of some broadcast or in the back of a newspaper under *human interest*, a term that's ironic as hell to me.

By the way, my name is Danny.

There's this old black man named Elsirus Cole. He's about eighty-three. He lives on a street called St. Aubin. He bought that house back in the 1960's and it was the proudest day of his life.

He fought in Korea, raised two kids and buried one wife, Martha, whose loss he's never recovered from. He refuses to move, even though his son and daughter beg him to each year.

He's not a very big man but he has these piercing eyes and very charming demeanor. Quick with a joke, calm of voice, in a word, he is cool, real cool and you just plain liked the guy when you met him.

Elsirus worked for The Ford Motor Company and retired with a full pension. Got a picture of himself with Henry Ford II at the plant on a goodwill tour that he keeps on his mantle.

He's lived to see the Tigers win three World Series and watch the city burn in race riots in 1943 and again in 1967. He lost a cousin and a sister in the last one, a bitter and terrible tragedy second only to the death of his wife from cancer.

After he retired, Elsirus started working with his church to counsel the city's wayward youth. This was his true calling. Mr. El, as he was called by the kids, was an avid reader, a fountain of history and knowledge and the kind of guy who always had an answer to any question, no matter how obscure or embarrassing.

He told stories that he had heard from his family, some of which went all the way back to sharecroppers, freed slaves and free men and women forced into slavery. All he had left of these people was a name, a man who was the first: Ochana.

Once, he even brought in a local writer who had made good, a man he often saw hanging out with the street people he wrote about. The kids didn't know who Dutch Leonard was or how lucky they were to meet him but that was a proud day for Mr. El.

Mr. El excelled in touching the lives of kids who had seen nothing but the worst of life in the city. Most of them went the normal path, to prison, early pregnancy, poverty or worse, the graveyard, but some he did get to, some lives, he saved and he often said that was a good thing.

And the ones who did get away from their troubles never forgot Mr. El and often came back to that little house to see him.

Which brings me to my violent beginning.

****

Ivory Shaw was what the brothers called a dime-piece. She was about five nine, had a beautiful, model-like face and a body that could stop traffic. She knew just how to dress so that her physical attributes were emphasized.

When she was around groups of men, she always made sure to give them a profile look at her, so they could see the swell of her breasts flow into her flat stomach and tiny waist and then her hips and ass explode from that narrow diameter. It made men crazy and she knew it.

But she wasn't one of those teasers who liked attention but then spurned every advance that came her way. Oh no, men loved Ivory and she loved them right back.

She was cool at leading them where she wanted them to go. But every once in a while, a guy would get too grabby or angry that she didn't just fall to her knees and blow him in public. These crazy ass men discovered that she had another side, a hard one that would find them picking up their faces or other body parts if it came to that.

Ivory was very different from her twin sister, Ivanna, who was also nice looking but hid her assets in favor of intellect. Ivanna became a teacher and never got in trouble. Ivory struggled to keep a job and seemed to always be in over her head.

Ivory was arrogant and willful. She became sexually active at twelve and fell in with the drug boys because of her looks. And even though she did well in school, it was far easier being a hot girl than a smart one. That's a no-brainer in the city.

She predictably fell in love with a nasty little piece of work named Raz Monty. He was what I called a Nowhere Man, a kid who was destined for prison or the graveyard. Drug addict mom, convict father and older brother, Raz never had a chance.

When a rival drug dealer inevitably killed Raz, Ivory fell apart and even her very large family could not help.

Ivory rebelled in school and was belligerent to everyone. That was a word she had never forgotten. It was almost her middle name for a few years. The juvie judge had said it to her in court where she faced sentencing for her third theft offense. She kinda knew what it meant and she embraced it. To Ivory, belligerent was a way of life.

She was sentenced to a youth center where she met Mr. El. She tried to antagonize him, to dismiss him, but Mr. El met every one of her bombs with one of his own.

"You know you want this old man," she'd say. "You'd have a damned heart attack."

"Don't seem like it's all that hard to get it from you," Mr. El would say. "You got change for this five?"

The old man gave her books to read, books about badass black women who didn't take shit but who always had noble hearts. He introduced her to Donald Goines and Pam Grier movies and let her see that it was okay to be a bad bitch as long as you were also a good one.

It took a while, but Mr. El won her over. Ivory was soon back in school and doing well. She was still belligerent but she saved it for those who deserved to see that side of her and she kept herself on the right side of the law— most of the time.

Mr. El smiled when he opened the heavy iron door to his house that day and saw who was on the other side.

"Look what the cat dragged in," said Mr. El.

"Hey, old man," said Ivory smiling.

"You come by yourself?" He asked in his smooth voice.

"It ain't even dark yet," said Ivory, then quickly correcting herself, "I mean, it isn't dark yet."

Mr. El didn't like slang or cursing unless it was in a movie or a book.

"Come on in," said Mr. El.

Ivory walked inside the familiar house and it was like a time warp. The decor was vintage, complete with a push button corded phone and a TV with dials and a remote.

In his living room, were three of his latest kids, two girls and a rough looking boy all about fifteen or so.

"Daaang," said the boy as he got a good look at Ivory who was wearing a jacket, tight jeans and boots.

"Hey everybody," said Ivory, ignoring the boy's comment. She did not want to encourage or insult him. Mr. El would throw her ass right out of the house if she did.

"These are my newbies," said Mr. El. That's Cyn, Zanevia and LaDamian.

"I didn't want to interrupt," said Ivory. "I just wanted to bring you this birthday card, cause I missed your party at the Center."

"Considerate, that's a good thing," said Mr. El taking the card. "Where'd you buy it?"

"You know I made it," said Ivory. "Mr. El doesn't like store bought cards," she said to the new kids.

"How old are you?" asked the girl named Cyn, an overweight kid with a quick smile.

"I'm eighty-three," said Mr. El with some pride.

The two girls both reacted with shock as Mr. El was very youthful looking.

"Mah berfday comin' up," said LaDamian in his heavy Detroit accent. "What I'm gon' get from you, shorty?"

Ivory frowned with disapproval, then looked at Mr. El who just smiled and nodded, giving some kind of approval.

"I got nothing for you," said Ivory. "Chances are, you be dead before the end of this or any year for that matter. Or you'll be one of them desperate niggas trying to rape some poor girl because he got no money and no game. I see you looking at all this chicken, thinking how good it is and you right, but it ain't for boys with one foot in the grave and not enough sense to step off."

The two girls wailed with laughter at LaDamian who dropped his head.

"What did I tell you about a worthy man, LaDamian?" asked Mr. El.

"He don't be hollerin' at bi-- uh, women. He talks to them with intelligence," said La Damian. "But I was just kiddin,' yo."

"Ivory, thanks for the card," said Mr. El. "Now, you get going before it gets dark. The Farmer chased off a drug crew but I don't think it took."

"The Farmer is bad!" said LaDamian. "I hear he been shot more time than Fiddy Cent."

"He's scary," said Cyn. Zanevia echoed this sentiment.

"Okay, Mr. El" said Ivory. "I'll see you next week. I want to ask you something. She added this with a lower register which alerted Mr. El's keen senses."

"You can do it here," said Mr. El. "It might teach these kids something."

"It's personal," said Ivory. "We'll talk. I promise."

Ivory said her goodbyes and walked out of the house. It was October and the sun was already falling fast. It was chilly and soon her jackets and boots would not be enough. She hated the Michigan winters and every year, she dreamt of living somewhere it was always warm.

Ivory got into her car, a little Toyota and pulled off. She had hoped Mr. El was alone. She'd planned to give him the card and then ask his advice about her problem but it could wait, she thought. Right now, she had it all under control. She had to teach some people respect but that was easy.

Her cell phone rang and it popped up on her car's display. It was RaRa, a dude that was all crazy in love with her. She liked him but she had given him some and the boy had lost his mind, talking like he wanted to get married.

RaRa was one of them computer boys and he made good money and she liked hanging out at his place but she could not see herself with him. He was too nice, too soft. She liked a different kind of man.

"'Sup RaRa?" she said after hitting the bluetooth button.

PROLOGUE: BELLIGERENT

"All good things," said RaRa whose voice was very smooth and mellow like Mr. El's. Too bad RaRa's looks didn't match that voice, she thought. "Lookin' to get with you tonight. Me and the crew going down to the Greektown Casino."

"On a weekday?"

"Thursday," said RaRa. "That's Negro Friday, woman."

This made Ivory laugh. He was funny, too. One more thing in his favor.

"I don't know," said Ivory. "My boss has been on me. One more time and she may fire my ass."

"Yo, Marcus is bringing his girl, Jelly. I want you to come to set her down."

Jelly was one of those girls Ivory hated. She had fake hair, fake titties and probably a fake ass. She was always name-dropping all the athletes she knew and even though all the guys knew she was a ho, they all just fell to their knees when she walked in jiggling her meat around.

"You know I hate that bitch," said Ivory.

"Me too. But whenever you come, she know she ain't the baddest one in the room and so she behaves herself."

"But I ain't even dressed up."

"Shit. You can put her down wearing nothing."

Ivory laughed again. RaRa didn't even get why that was funny but she did. "Okay, but you payin' and my ass his hun-gray."

"Bet," said RaRa.

Suddenly, Ivory heard the short blast of a police car's siren. She pulled over and took the phone off the bluetooth.

"What the fuck?" said Ivory. RaRa's face popped up on her display.

"Keep me on the line," said RaRa. "Them muthafuckas be trippin' these days."

"No worries," said Ivory. "I got it."

"Oh, it's your sister's man."

"Naw, it ain't him. It's... Look, I'll see you at what time?"

"Nine, Greektown," said RaRa.

"Cool."

The facts are sketchy after this but we know Ivory was taken to the 11th Precinct and the next day, she was found dead in a cell at 5:35 am. The cause of death was asphyxiation by strangulation.

Her family was notified. One of them was her sister, Vinny Shaw, a lawyer, ex-cop and the mother of my son.

PART ONE:

LIFE CITY

"When a man's got vulnerabilities,
you can make him do anything."

- Renardo

1

WHITE KID, DARK LIFE

Every day, I want to hurt somebody. Not literally, unless you count my next-door neighbor, who I really would like to shoot because he is really annoying.

I'm not going crazy, I'm just pissed about a lot of shit, injustice mostly, little things like how they tell you that you can do anything in this country, when they know all the odds are against you and how they give false hope to poor people, when if you are born poor, you will probably die poor.

And who are *they*? Well, in the black community *they* are a special, select group of people who have controlled life for ages.

They are the reason you have a job and the reason you will never make any money at it. *They* are the ones who own your sports team and the ones who fix the games. *They* sell dope then arrest you for it, then make it legal but keep you from making legit money on it. *They* are evil and there's nothing your ass can do about it.

This is the kind of shit I can't get out of my head and probably why I became a cop. I can do something about *them*, only just a little at a time.

I am white, Irish actually, which to me is not really white. And I don't mean this like that crazy woman who pretended to be black. What I mean is, Irish people are the black people of white people. Check your history if you don't believe me.

But I don't sound like a white man. I sound like a black one. I picked up the voice living in one of Detroit's worst neighborhoods. It's not an imitation and it's not a put on. It's just who I am.

I got some size on me as the old heads say and so pretty much I don't get messed with, that and I carry two guns, a Glock and a S&W .45 ACP, which my shrink said reflected my inner and outer conflicts.

Yeah, I used to see a shrink but like I said, I ain't going crazy. I had a few issues but it's all behind me now, mostly.

I live with a woman named Vinny Shaw. She was my partner when I was in uniform. She is a beautiful woman, a dime like her unfortunate sister.

I was almost kicked off the force when a guy shot Vinny at a Big Boy Restaurant and I damned near beat him to death. The crowd cheered me on and I broke both hands. By the way, that guy got better, sued the city, won some money and was killed for it by some of his friends. Hashtag, justice.

Me and Vinny just had a son, Robert Marcus Cavanaugh, who we call The Notorious RMC and is close to a year old now. He's a great kid, smiles a lot, though he must get that from Vinny. And I know he's a miracle because when I see him, I don't want to hurt anybody.

PART ONE: LIFE CITY

It's true that you never appreciate your parents until you have kids. Well, now I do and I can see just how tough my parents' generation was, how much they sacrificed for us and how sad it is for them to see things change as they are dying.

We're all a bunch of pussies now. Whining and crying about our hurt feelings for every little thing that happens. Our parents and their parents before them didn't do that, too busy worrying about having food and not freezing to death each winter.

My mother, Lucy was a racist who killed herself because she suffered from clinical depression and no one knew what the hell that was back then. She also died of a broken heart because she saw her little boy corrupted by the dark people she despised and watched him disappear into a culture where she was not wanted and did not want to be.

In her damaged mind, it was all this terrible, evil thing that was after her and in the end, she was right because it killed her.

My father, Robert, was a drunk who despite not being a bigot was nonetheless a hard man who wanted me to be as tough as I could be.

He was the man who walked through my elementary school in full uniform and dropped me into an all-black classroom. Lets just say, there were many scuffles after that.

I'm tough but at a considerable price. I have buried many friends and I've sent several well-deserving lowlives to an early grave. It has left me cold and empty inside, a trait that serves me well as a detective in Detroit but is a struggle in everything else.

It's good in a way to see the worse in order to prevent the worst from happening to innocent people. At least, that's what I tell myself.

My first days in that all black neighborhood were pretty bad. I was some combination of black and blue all the time. And yet, I never felt resentful of all the black people, just the assholes who are pretty much like the white ones.

The neighborhood itself was working class. Most of the men worked for the car companies one way or another. You could tell which one by the car they drove, usually. A lot of families struggled and many only had a mother.

There were a lot of churches, big ones with huge congregations and smaller ones, wedged in tiny storefronts or converted offices that usually had names that tried to make up for their size. My favorite was The Lord's Holy Cathedral of Righteous and Divine Fellowship.

My family traveled across town to go to Mass at St. Joseph's but every once in a while, I went to the black church. My mother never went of course, but my father encouraged it.

If you've never been to black church service, you need to go. It's an experience if the place is on their game. Good music, good food and good fellowship. Only thing is, they try to keep you there all damned day, like prison.

The houses in the 'hood were small, wood-framed boxes that were close together and you had better hope you liked your neighbors because they would know all your business and you would know theirs.

The people were mostly from the South and many of the older ones still had Mississippi, Georgia or Texas in their voices. The Detroit accent is a combination of these and a Midwestern twang that's very distinctive.

I made a friend, a good one, who is still my best friend today. I often feel Jazzy Jeff to his Fresh Prince but that's okay. He is allowed to be great because we were each other's lifelines back in the day.

Marshall Jackson is a handsome, brilliant and now wealthy attorney. I could hate him for that but we have always been an odd fit, a round peg that somehow was always supposed to go into the square hole.

We fought side by side in school. I was persecuted for being white and he was persecuted for not persecuting me. Still don't know why he decided to risk his life to be my friend. I guess he's just good like that.

And then one day, all my troubles turned around when I fought this kid we called Koney.

Koney was as big as a man. He'd been left back twice and so he was almost fourteen when he began to terrorize me.

I had the great misfortune to like a girl that Koney also liked, a pretty little thing named Pricilla. She was dark brown and had the biggest, brownest eyes I'd ever seen. She always smelled nice, like fresh flowers and she spoke with a bit of an accent which made the other girls hate her.

All my girlfriends have been black. I know that sounds strange, but it isn't really for most black kids in the inner city. And though I am white, I was indoctrinated just like all the other boys to the ways of the world and in that world, the sisters were everything.

Well, after a month of begging, I finally got to walk with Pricilla after school. Her mother liked me and her father did too, which almost never happened. And one Saturday, while visiting her at home, she kissed me goodbye, a little peck on the lips that I can still feel sometimes.

That innocent kiss was not just love and sex but acceptance by the culture that had kept me out for so long.

Marshall was impressed. He always had at least one girlfriend but looked officially jealous of me for the first time.

It wasn't long before I heard that Koney was looking to fight me over taking his woman. I didn't want to fight him because I thought I'd lose and it's not like in the movies where a guy gets beat up and the girl runs to him. In Detroit, you lose a fight and you get ridiculed, made fun of and no one wants to be around you.

I thought it was better not to avoid him and so I went looking for him. He wasn't hard to find. He was always behind the school near the dumpsters smoking discarded cigarettes or something else he had no business doing. This day, he was in the parking lot.

I walked up and just stood there. Koney laughed with his two rough-looking friends whose names I can never remember, although one of them would later be killed by a citizen in an attempted carjacking.

"Shoulda ran home, white boy," said Koney, dropping the butt he held in his hand.

I said nothing. I'd had a lot of fights by now and I knew talking was just a lot of nothing.

Most fights didn't last very long. My father had been teaching me hand to hand and giving me instruction that often left me hurting pretty bad.

I had been fighting my father in practice and on the street for real for years now and when you do anything enough, you get good at it. Well, I was going to find out if all my training had amounted to anything.

Koney waded in, doing karate sounds and acting silly to the delight of the crowd that had assembled. Marshall was behind me ready to get into it if the friends tried to jump me.

"Yo ass gonna be red as fuck, white boy," said Koney raising his fists.

I raised my hands and watched his eyes and matched his foot movement.

Koney feinted a punch but I did not flinch. His eyes, told me he was not going to attack.

Suddenly, he rushed at me, hoping to catch me off guard, knock me down and just sit on me and beat me down. This was how most fights were won, with speed and size.

It didn't work. I moved to one side and Koney shot by me, lost his footing and fell on his face.

The crowd gasped and the girls laughed. That was all it took for Koney to become enraged. He got up and stalked toward me as if I were nothing and would just let him grab then beat me.

He shot out a hand to do just that. I knocked it away and hit him as hard as I could in his gut. He grabbed his middle and cursed. Before he could recover, I raised my head into his chin, snapping his head back. Then I punched him in the throat. He grabbed his neck and he bent forward, choking. I pulled his head down into my knee and broke his nose. He fell backward, blood gushing from his face. He didn't get up because I fell on him and just beat at his face until my hands were covered with blood.

One of the friends tried to jump me but Marshall tripped him and he fell on his ass. The other friend took off running. When the other one got up, he wanted no parts of a fight.

I finally got off Koney after he begged me. I stood and kicked him right in the nuts and he spit out an arc of blood that made the crowd gasp.

My hands were dripping blood and I felt good. Hell, I felt great. I think that was the first time I really enjoyed a fight. And knowing the code of the street, I raised by bloody hand, pointed to him and said:

"Next time, you die."

After that, I was king shit at school. Someone started a rumor that I was crazy and on medication. Another story was that I had ripped his ear off with my teeth.

Around the neighborhood, I was challenged. I won some and lost some but soon I was unafraid of anyone and once you get there, no one bothers you, really.

My father was called to the school but I was never in trouble, in fact, he was very proud of me and gave me a taste of a beer he was drinking. Hashtag, Irish.

And Pricilla, well, we broke up that summer as soon as something better came along because that's how kids are.

There were many other innocent crushes until I met Pamela Tinsley. I was only fifteen and she was nineteen, although she seemed older. Pam was a fun girl and known to give it up without a lot of drama.

I was actually after another girl in the neighborhood, a local track star named Nerva Wallis. But her mother was a bible toting Christian and that ass was locked up like a bank. That's what some of the guys called her behind her back. Still, I did like her and so I tried to get next to her but it was rough going. No man can compete with Jesus.

Pam lived on the same street as Nerva and had her own place in the family's garage out back. She worked in a restaurant and paid rent to her folks who knew she was one stroke away from having their grandchild and so they at least wanted to keep her close.

One evening after dropping Nerva from seeing a movie, where all I got were some kisses and a few feels in the dark theater, I was summoned by Pamela who was leaning out of her window in that converted garage.

"Where you comin' from Danny?" she asked sweetly.

"My girl's place," I said proudly.

"You mean that stiff ass Nerva the virgin?"

"Yeah, but she fine though."

"Uh huh. You a virgin, too Danny?"

"Hell naw," I lied. "You know I be gettin' mine, Pam."

"I know," she said with what I would call a delicious smile. "Why don't you go over to Jo Ann's and get me a combo? I'll split it with you."

"For real?" I said. Jo Ann's Barbecue was no joke and I was hungry. "Bet."

She gave me the money and I was back with a big bag filled with food. I went inside that little garage and she had a bottle of liquor opened up and was drinking.

Now every man has what I call pussy radar. It sounds when you realize your chances of getting some are pretty good. Pam was drinking. She had music playing and not just any music, the Isley Brothers' "Footsteps In The Dark," old school and now we had some food. I got an erection as soon as I walked in.

Pam was wearing a low cut top that showed off her breasts and a skirt that was way too short. She was a fine piece of womanhood and I had often fantasized about her but she only dated grown ass men and just teased us little guys.

I put the food down and she offered me a drink. I took it because I didn't want to be rude and you know, I am Irish.

I sipped the brown liquor and we ate the ribs and then she began to talk about some man she was doing and how he had broken up with her over some dumb shit.

Next thing I know, she got her hand on my leg. I'm complimenting her, telling her how good she looks and how any man would have to be crazy to leave her.

"You really like that Nerva the bank girl?" she asked.

"Yeah, I do," I said and regretted it as soon as I said it. "But you know she ain't a woman like you."

"You know Danny, I don't think you could lie if you wanted to. That's a good quality for a man."

"Not all the time," I said truthfully.

"It is with me," said Pam "I know you like her but she's gonna keep you waiting for that. Ain't right to keep men waiting."

"I know how she is but I ain't trying to gank her for it. I ain't like that."

"No, you're not," said Pam smiling again. "You'd think this rotten ass neighborhood would have broken you by now but you're still here. You and that Marshall."

She leaned back on the sofa we were sitting on and I took this to mean maybe she was done talking and I'd have to go. I was already thinking I could weave this little adventure into a nice lie about getting some and then Pam pulled down her top letting me see her breasts, which were damned near perfect.

"What do you think of me?" she asked. "I know you won't lie."

I had a hard time finding my voice and I remember it cracking a little.

"You cool. Everybody knows you fine as hell. Some of the fellas they say you a ho but they just mad cause you ain't feelin' them. Girls don't like you unless they fine too, because you have their men staring at you and shit. I saw my dad looking one day. That was weird as fuck."

She laughed and her breasts jiggled nicely. She moved across the little sofa and kissed me. My hands went right for her breasts. I grabbed them and pushed her on her back and got on top of her. We kissed for a while and then she pushed me back. I was about to explode and I didn't know what I had done wrong.

"It'll be better in the bed," she said.

We walked into a room that had been made by a wall her father had put up and there was a bed and a bathroom in the back.

"I know you ain't had none," said Pam. "So, I'm gonna show you how. You gonna come fast the first time but that's okay. The second time, we'll take it slower."

We got naked and I just stared at her, not believing my luck. She was perfect in her proportions and not that skinny ass body they show on TV. She was Serena Williams like perfect, thick and round and firm.

Pam pulled a condom out of a drawer I suspected was filled with them. I took it and got it on, almost blind with desire.

And then, the best thing of all. Any man will tell you that he never forgets when a women surrenders to him the first time. It is a moment of triumph and elation, a time when you are vulnerable and powerful at the same time.

Pam moved back in the bed and parted her legs and held out her hand.

"Come on," she said.

I climbed into bed and had no trouble finding her. The heat of that first connection was electric. I said something, although I can't remember what and I started pumping and when I came, I thought all of my insides would empty out of me.

Turns out I lasted about five minutes, not bad considering it was my first time at bat. Well, Pam and I more than made up for that the second and third times. I wore her out, or she wore me out. In any event, I didn't get home until well after eleven, which got me a stiff arm from my father. I gladly took it and never stopped smiling.

There were many girlfriends after that summer, all black and all pretty. I saw white girls who I thought were nice but see, there's this thing about black women, this heavy, savory, kind of sexuality that just commands your desire and once you get it, well, you're kinda spoiled for anything else.

And don't get the feeling that I was some kind of favorite with the sisters. I wasn't. For every black girl that dared to like me, there were ten who wouldn't touch me if I was covered with money and pie. If they did, they were called a slut, a ho or a race traitor. I know that sounds bad, but all I can say is, white people were probably doing the same thing to black boys.

I see all these really rich white men with black wives and I get it. They can do whatever they want without judgment and so they just go for what they've always been wanting. I do too. I just didn't need the money to get there.

Marshall was trippin' after I told him about Pam that summer. I found out that with all the girlfriends he had that he was still a virgin. We had both been lying about it but he was happy for me.

I told him how good it was and how I was learning stuff. He lost his own virginity later that year and since then, we have both been as thick as thieves in that department.

We went to high school where Marshall played basketball and I played baseball. I was a first baseman and had a batting average of .405, pretty good but I was slow and not good enough to get scouted by the Tigers.

I kicked around after school doing odd jobs and avoiding the police academy. Then I joined the Marines. I thought my father would lose it but he was jumping for joy.

What shocked me was when Marshall quit college and joined me. This damned near killed his mother. By then, his dad was dead (a crime that was solved by my father) his sister was on drugs and his brother, Moses was deep into crime. I think that's why he did it, to get away from all that shit.

We did our stint and came home. Marshall went back to college and I went into the Police Academy.

I loved being a cop but I had a bad temper and a penchant for violence. I still hold a record for OIS

(Officer Involved Shootings) and I am second only to a man named Nickerson for men put down. I used to be proud of that but these days, I prefer to solve problems with my brain.

I love my city as only a kid with my background can. We have some bad history but we're far from over. You may have heard that Detroit went belly up, filed the biggest bankruptcy in the history of life. Now the city was on the mend, but it's also on the grind.

Grinding means working every angle, fair and unfair legal and illegal to get ahead. The businessmen are grinding, getting tax breaks and making money off folks. The criminals are always on the grind and they are staking out new scams and deals but enforced the same old way, by violence.

We even got us a new mayor, a white one. Shit shocked the hell out of me but it makes sense. The last one dragged the collective will of the people into a gutter. I helped to send his ass away, so I shed not one tear for him. I guess folks got tired of black mayors and wanted to give a white guy a try and yes, he's grinding, too.

On the street, some still call me Danny Two Gun because I used both weapons in a firefight. The brothers respect a man that kicks ass and so, I have many street contacts who are loyal to me even though cops are getting a bad rep lately.

A lot of cops like the power but don't understand that it flows both ways. You can't be pissed when someone doesn't respect you and you can't be afraid to take an ass whipping if it comes to that.

PART ONE: LIFE CITY

Don't really know what else to tell you. My favorite color is green. I like to drink beer and whiskey. I love soul food but I can't cook worth a shit but I think I can. My favorite Faygo flavor is orange, I love White Castles but they don't love me and I bleed Tiger orange and blue.

There is one last thing to know about me. Having lived in the 'hood for so long under very tense circumstances, I learned to be very observant. You will find this to be a common trait of many innercity types. Knowing when to run and when to avoid danger can be the difference between living and dying.

So, I notice things, things that sometimes black folks don't see because they're black and white folks don't see because they're white.

I am both and neither.

I see everything.

2

<u>GRIEF TEAM</u>

The Shaw house on Outer Drive was surrounded by the local and national media. All the major networks were represented and their reporters chattered in different areas, trying to act as though they were the only media present.

Freelance paparazzi roamed like little snakes, trying to get shots of the family. One man had come into the backyard and gotten a rock thrown at him.

I had called some cop friends to back them off, but they could only be made to stay so far away. Also, we all had to turn off all of our phones as they would not stop ringing or vibrating from friends calling.

These kinds of police involved murders were national news lately and now the eyes of the world were on Vinny and her family. Another unarmed black person killed at the hands of police raised all of the ugliness of our history and gave people a reason to tap the anger we all held behind our logic and political correctness.

I heard that my name had come up on MSNBC. They talked about how odd it was to have a cop in the black family who was married to a white cop who was known to be violent.

Some asshole named Chris Hayes even made a joke about how he wouldn't want to be at our house on Thanksgiving.

Me and Vinny are not married and they conveniently left out all the times I have saved people's asses and how I once helped catch the killer of a Supreme Court Justice. Also, I did not like the picture of me they used. They always try to make cops look mean and crazy.

The Notorious RMC seemed oblivious to all of the grief around him. People were crying, wailing and usually, a baby picks up on that and starts crying too. But not my son. He was not smiling and did not seem particularly happy, but he was not given to grief as we all mourned the passing of Ivory Shaw. Boy is definitely a Cavanaugh.

Vinny held the baby and tried not to cry as her father gave the clan the bad news about Ivory.

Vinny was from a family of ten kids. They were in order, Renitta, the oldest, Juan, (pronounced jew-wan) Ivory and Ivanna, the twins, DeWayne, Easter, Teyron, Devinna and Marcus Jr.

Even Vinny has trouble keeping them all apart in her head sometimes. Now, in the grief-stricken house of her father, I couldn't tell who was who as they were all crying or in some stage of breakdown or anger. Black folk, like the Irish, do not believe in holding in grief. All of it is let out until there is nothing left but spirit.

Vinny's mother kept passing out and so she was in another room and sedated. The men all raged with thoughts of revenge and the women all huddled together just as angry, but trying to keep calm heads.

PART ONE: LIFE CITY

For a family their size, it was actually pretty good that only one person had died from violence. This was a testament to good parenting and faith. In most black families this big, at least two of the men would have been dead by now or in prison. In truth, the Shaw family had been quite lucky.

But now was not the time to bring up some shit like that. White people have a bad habit of saying well-intentioned things like this that come off as ignorant or arrogant. And so I did what I usually did at family gatherings, I shut the fuck up and did what everyone else was doing, in this case, I was grieving.

I wasn't worried about Vinny's family doing violence, except in the case of Juan Shaw. He seemed harmless but I knew better. Juan was just very smart and had hidden all of his extracurricular activities over the years. He'd sold drugs and been involved with a low level gang. He was clever and had gotten out in time.

He worked for GM in quality control and had a couple of kids by a couple of ladies. Juan was a hard, tough bastard who loved the twins and had practically raised them with Renitta.

"Let me holla 'atcha for a second," I'd said to Juan earlier. I'd made it a point to do this as soon as I came in not wanting to waste any time.

Juan was angry, still breathing a little hard and his eyes were narrowed slits. You could not fake that look. That's how a man looked when wanted to do you harm.

"You know me, Juan," I'd said. "You know I'm an honest man, a good cop."

"We know that, Danny," said Juan. "We don't hold nothin' against you on this. But we know there's some dirty damned dogs in there with you. Look at what they're doing to us."

"Yeah, we got some rot inside these days. Look, I know you wanna kill this man, whoever he is," I said. "Believe me, if he was here now, I'd just turn my back, right after I handed you my gun."

Juan laughed darkly. "Yeah and it wouldn't take me long neither."

"Me and Vinny are the cops but everybody's gonna be looking at you and your daddy, you know. I ain't asking you to calm down or none of that shit. Anger is good right now. Just be smooth about it, measured. We want this dude caught. After that, I don't care what happens to him."

"I feel you on that," said Juan. "I usually look to daddy but he's gettin' old and I know this has hit him hard. He feels like he's done good, none of us dying or going to jail all these years."

"He has," I said, glad he brought it up.

"I know I need to step up," said Juan. "Last thing we need is for this lowlife to get off because of something one of us did."

"It's on you this time." I said. "If you need me, just ask anything, anytime. You know me and Vinny will get it for you."

We hugged and I could feel some of his rage going away as he realized that he had to be a voice of reason.

PART ONE: LIFE CITY

Honestly, I didn't know if it had worked. I didn't want him to go back to his old ways and maybe catch a bullet.

Marcus Jr. was young and could be a bit of a hothead too, but the family had very high hopes for him. He was a big, good-looking kid who was a star athlete and so no one was going to let him do anything stupid. I let that one slide.

Ivory Shaw never liked me much. I never knew why. I guess it was the white thing.

When Vinny and I had a big fight a year ago, Ivory was right in the middle of it, volunteering to take Vinny in as she walked out on me. I'd never forgotten the look on Ivory's face back then. She might as well had written *fuck you* on her forehead.

Ivory kept her distance from me even as her twin and I became close. Ivanna had held my hand so tight, that I thought she would hurt me.

It was odd for everyone seeing Ivanna who looked so much like her dead sister. And for Ivanna, she'd lost part of herself and it was never coming back.

I was very sad about it all. I'd seen my share of death but no girl that young and beautiful deserved to die and by the hand of a cop. But I knew Ivory had a mouth on her and did not walk away from confrontations.

I was already planning to talk to Mr. El and her friends to see what they knew. I knew the normal path would be to look at the police but that would get me nothing until I could pull some leverage from her life.

PART ONE: LIFE CITY

See, I was way ahead of the people looking into this murder. I knew the victim and I knew she was probably into some unsavory, if not illegal shit and that would lead me right back to the cop that did this.

Her car had not been found and we were looking for it. I had a feeling that we'd never find it. A cop knows how to get rid of evidence and so that car was probably long gone.

The police were not trying to say Ivory had killed herself. That would have been ridiculous as no one could strangle themselves. But there was no record of Ivory having been brought in or processed.

Internal Affairs was on the case as well as the U.S. Attorney and the FBI. The Black Lives Matter people were already in town and on the news. Vinny's family had told them that they would not be making any statements with them.

This was Marcus Shaw Sr.'s doing. He was an old school cat and he did not like grandstanding in the face of tragedy. He was more concerned with a proper funeral, his church and Ivory's immortal soul.

Renitta, Vinny's oldest sister and the one who disliked me the most, made it a point to pull us both aside and share her thoughts and grief. I didn't care for her much but I could see she was really hurting.

Ivory was one of Renitta's favorites and she had shepherded Ivory through a lot of trouble and was the one who had introduced her to Mr. El. For Renitta, who had no kids of her own and one adopted cousin, this was like losing a daughter.

"You gotta find out who did this," said Renitta wiping away the tears. "He can't get away with this. Fucking dirty ass cops."

"We'll do what we can," said Vinny, "but when it's cops, it's handled by IAD and the Feds."

"Then we should get a P.I., a good one," said Renitta. "I don't trust cops of any kind now."

Vinny looked at me with that wife look when she does not want you to say something to make a bad situation worse. Our hands were tied but Renitta and probably the rest of the family, didn't want to hear that. They had two cops in the family and they wanted results.

"We will find out who did it," I said. "We'll bring them in to stand trial."

Renitta finally stopped crying. Vinny was giving me that look again but I was cool.

"Good," said Renitta. "Daddy!" she called to Marcus Sr. who came over. She told him what I had just said and the old man looked at me with wide eyes.

"You think you can do that?" he asked his voice full of hope. "I don't want nobody to get hurt. We've suffered enough."

"He's just trying to be nice," said Vinny. "We will keep the family abreast of everything we know."

"I meant it, Vinny," I said. "You know how the fellas are. They're going to close ranks, even though Ivory is related to a cop. You and me will be pushed out but we both have friends who can help us."

"When can we have her body?" asked Marcus Sr. "We need to get her buried."

"I don't know sir," I said. "Forensics has her and I know Fiona is doing the duty. I need to get to her ASAP to find out what she knows. And as soon as I do, you will know. But the family has to control information. If people find out me and Vinny are working this, we're all finished."

"Don't worry," said Marcus Sr. "We got it."

He took Renitta by the shoulder and started talking to her as he led her away. Vinny was still staring at me and I knew we'd have words but then Marshall and his wife hit the door.

Chemin Jackson was red-eyed and Marshall didn't look much better as they entered and began hugging everyone.

Chemin was just the kind of woman you'd expect to be married to a man who was going to be a legend one day. She was gorgeous, smart and as tough as they came.

After saying hello to everyone, Marshall and Chemin made a beeline to me and Vinny.

"The FBI is watching this but they haven't decided how deep they want to get into it," said Marshall not bothering with niceties.

"Usually, they just want total credit," I said.

"Can I hold the baby?" asked Chemin, still sniffling a little. Vinny smiled and handed him over.

"We didn't want to bring the kids," said Marshall.

"Tell them about the mayor," said Chemin.

"He's got a special taskforce working on the cops," said Marshall. "Chief Hill is heading it up. Not going to be good for the men in the eleventh."

"They'll break them all up," said Vinny. "That's what they did when they had that problem in the fifth. Chopped up the whole bunch and spread them all over. Fired some, too."

"Are you guys going to make a statement?" asked Chemin, wrestling with the baby. "Everyone's waiting on it."

"It's up to daddy," said Vinny. "Personally, I don't care."

"I wouldn't," said Marshall. "The killer's still out there, and you know he's watching everything. We don't want to do anything that might make him more careful."

"What's the county's take on all this?" I asked.

"They want blood, of course," said Marshall. "And before you ask, I would never defend anyone in a case like this."

When the old mayor was arrested because I found evidence on him, he had hired Marshall and put us on opposite sides of the case. I didn't want to go through that again and apparently neither did Marshall.

"Somebody's gotta know who did it," said Chemin. "I mean, they're cops and there are only so many. They wouldn't cover for a killer, would they?"

"Yes," said Vinny and I agreed with her.

"I know it sounds harsh," said Marshall, "but it's a thing with them, just like lawyers know who's guilty and never tell."

"I couldn't do that," said Chemin giving Vinny the baby back. "I couldn't live with myself."

"I'm gonna go and talk with your father, Vinny," said Marshall. "I know it's early, but all of you need to start thinking about the lawsuit. Ivory was technically in police custody and so the city's on the hook. And now, with the publicity, they will not want a lawsuit."

Marshall walked off and Chemin followed after kissing RMC on the forehead. As soon as they were gone, I could feel eyes on me again.

"Go on and say it," I said.

"Danny, why would you promise to get the killer? You know how hard it's going to be," said Vinny shifting the baby.

"I know who's gonna get the case in IAD and she will give me some latitude," I said.

"Gomez?" said Vinny after a moment of thought.

Vinny was not prone to jealousy, but DeAngela Gomez in IAD got to her. DeAngela was a lead investigator for the rat squad and had once been on my case. She had also let it be known that she had a crush on me back in the day. I was not interested but that made no difference to Vinny who had seen a picture of DeAngela in the news and taken an instant dislike to her.

"Yes, it's DeAngela," I said.

Vinny said nothing but brooded. I didn't push it because that was our way. She was mad and sifting through her insecurities, which had grown some since the baby. If we were a normal couple, I would have pointed out how she went into work wearing them tight ass dresses all the time and said it was for work when I knew damned well she got off on showing men her body.

Vinny knew how unfaithful most cops were and though we had proven to be the exception, that made no difference. A baby changed everything and not all of it was good. Once a woman had a child, she felt a little less attractive somehow and no matter how much her man tries to play up that she's still got it, the woman always feels that something is lacking.

"I'll work the political side," said Vinny after a while. "The firm's partners are well connected."

"It's going to be tricky for me. My boss has to be down with it but I'm good to go."

Vinny just nodded and handed the baby to me. He yawned and it made me yawn. His little eyes fluttered and I could tell he was starting to go down. That was good, because I had work to do.

3

COLD

I left my house the next day and the first winter wind hit me. It was like a knife across my face. It had been cold since September but this was the first sign winter was coming, that icy, jagged invisible hand that just freezes everything in its path.

I pulled up my collar and went to my car. The media had my house staked out too, so one of the news crews followed me. It was easy to shake him and soon I was out on my own and on my way to see Mr. El.

It was a trek across town to the old neighborhood just outside of Hamtramck, which had just made news as the first American city to become majority Muslim. Funny to see women in *berkas* and *hijab* walking outside of the old Polish businesses and rustic homes.

I arrived to find Mr. El's place surrounded by more of the media. A couple of news vans were outside of his home. I rolled past, parked up the street, then doubled back after calling him to let me in the backdoor ,which he did.

"Sorry about all this," I said as I came in. The little house was warm and I felt the chill fade away from by bones.

"No problem," said Mr. El. "They've been out there for two days now, trying to talk to me. Newspaper's been calling too, but I'm not interested. They even had Mitch Albom call 'cause they know he's my favorite but I had to turn him down."

"You don't mind talking to me do you?" I asked.

"'Course not," said Mr. El.

And for the first time, I could see he'd been crying.

"I'm trying to get to the bottom of all this," I said. "Did you see anything when she came here to see you?"

"No, she came by, gave me a birthday card, then left and that was it. Next I heard, she was gone. Just like that."

"Did she tell you anything that might be important, any secrets about men or cops she was seeing?" I asked.

"She was always seeing some man or another," said Mr. El. "Girl just could not say no to a man if he bowed to her power. I told her not to be so free with herself but you know Ivory."

"What about her friends?" I asked "We got a list of them but did she ever talk about them?"

"All the time. Lately, she was liking this boy named Raymond. They call him RaRa. Met him once at the center. He was a nice boy and I could tell he was real taken with Ivory. Followed her around like a puppy. He's one of them IT guys. Smart as a whip and funny. I told her that's the kinda boy she needed but I could see Ivory didn't want him, didn't respect that kind of love. She could only get excited about dangerous men."

"Was she involved with a cop to your knowledge?"

"No but she did say she wanted to talk to me about something that night. But I had guests and she didn't feel comfortable telling it in front of them. That could have been it."

I said nothing. I was thinking about RaRa. The police had already moved to question him and his crew of friends but so far, I hadn't heard anything.

"Ivory had been with a man, a married one, last year," said Mr. El. "I was mad as hell about it but she told it to me in confidence. It went on for a while and then he dumped her. She was pissed and did some of that crazy woman stuff."

"Like phone calls, stalking him?" I asked.

"Yes," said Mr. El. "I told her that was beneath her but—"

"I know Ivory," I finished for him. "Got a name?"

"Bakersfield," said Mr. El. "He's a doctor, got that big east side practice, MidCiti Medical."

"I've seen the commercials," I said.

"I'm tired," said Mr. El. "This city just eats and eats at you until there's nothing left. My family's been asking me to come to Florida for years. Think I'm gonna take them up on it. People are buying up houses now that the city's making a comeback. I could get a few bucks for this shack and just go."

"We'd miss you," I said. "We need good men here."

"I'm old," said Mr. El. "Everyday I get a little more afraid. It's especially bad in the winter. You know, in some countries, an old man is revered, here he's a mark, just waiting for some coward to jump him."

I couldn't disagree with him. My father was getting on and I worried about him each day.

PART ONE: LIFE CITY

"Thanks for your time," I said. "If you think of anything, call me."

"I will," said Mr. El. "When's the funeral?"

"I don't know. The city still has the body. Might be a while."

"Too bad she wasn't Jewish. They have to get their dead buried quick."

I thanked the old man again and left by the back entrance. I looked out on the desolate streets and I could feel it, change was coming to the city. This neighborhood would soon be something else, an industrial park, a gentrified residence or a business district. *They* would move the black folks out and then build something great and ban common folk from using it and the world would just keep spinning.

More cold air greeted me as I turned a corner. There were many kinds of cold in the North. What was cold to a Texan we'd laugh at in Michigan, but talk to someone from Canada about cold.

For me, the change of seasons had meaning. There was less crime when it got cold but the things that did happen always seemed to be worse and every spring thaw, we'd find something bad that had been laying all winter.

I got into my car and headed out further east. Dr. Bakersfield was a lead I bet the cops didn't have.

Ivory's phone wasn't found on her and she didn't have a computer or a tablet. Like a lot of young kids without a lot of money, her phone contained her digital life.

The cops were probably getting all of her online information now but I was betting that they'd find nothing. Ivory was a secretive girl and way too smart to leave a trail of her activities for the public. All they'd find would be a lot harmless crap and selfies of her in provocative outfits.

MidCiti Medical was one of those Detroit success stories you never read about. Some kids got out of medical school and started an inner city practice, catering to the failing health of the underclass. That led to the state backing them with money for wellness programs and then the big one, Obamacare.

The exchanges blew up their business and soon the four friends had a big facility near a hospital and a partnership with Wayne Medical, one of the country's best medical schools.

Dr. Paul Bakersfield was a graduate of WSU and one of its most illustrious alumni. It didn't take me long to spot him in the facility as I had seen him on his TV spots. Also, he towered over his staff at six foot seven. He'd been a lousy basketball player but it had helped pay the school bills for his real talent.

He was a handsome man, definitely Ivory's type, forties, salt and pepper hair, good build and a very snappy dresser. I was no fashion expert, but I knew a good pair of shoes when I saw them and the ones he sported were at least three hundred.

I waited until the crowd around him thinned, then I flashed my badge and asked to speak to him in private.

"What's this about?" asked Bakersfield.

"A murder case," I said flatly and before he said anything, I saw the familiar look at the sound of my voice then a flash of fear. He was my man.

"Not anyone I know I hope," said Bakersfield, trying to cover his anxiety.

"I'm afraid it is," I said. "Which is why I wanted to speak in private."

"I don't think so," said Bakersfield. "I have lots of lawyers. You can talk to them." He turned to leave.

"If you want," I said. "But my next stop is your wife. We can talk about Ivory Shaw."

This got his attention. He stopped and for a moment, stood with his back to me. No one around us suspected anything and they just kept working, walking by Bakersfield and saying hello. He stood there at a crossroads in his life. Then, he turned back to me.

"Let's speak in my office," he said.

He walked me to the other side of the place, where the partners had their offices in each corner.

Bakersfield's office faced downtown. I came in and took a seat in a leather chair that faced his desk.

"Make yourself at home," said Bakersfield. "Can I get you anything?"

"Scotch and water, hold the scotch," I said.

Bakersfield grabbed two bottles of water from his bar on the other side of the room.

"I heard about that girl," said Bakersfield.

"Ivory Shaw," I said. "You can deny you know her," I said, "but that will just lead me back to your wife and then the police and the newspapers. So far, no one in the investigation knows that you knew her."

I could see him contemplating what to do. If he lied, then all hell would break loose but if he came clean to me, then another person knew and I could be looking to blackmail him for what I knew. And then there was the matter of proof. Did I have any and if so, what was it, how damning?

"I heard what happened to her," said Bakersfield. "I had nothing to do with it."

"I don't know that," I said. "You were fucking her, leading her on and she took revenge on you. Maybe you got mad or maybe your wife found out."

"The police killed her. It's on the news and Ivory and I hadn't seen each other for months."

"I need the story, all of it," I said," or I take what I know and the pictures to your wife."

I had no pictures but young girls love to take them and I knew Ivory had to have at least one pic of this asshole on her phone.

He told me how he'd met Ivory at the youth center giving a seminar on health care. He'd flirted and she flirted right back and it wasn't long before they were meeting in hotels. He was giving her money and telling her that he wanted to leave his wife for her.

Ivory took the bait, probably desperate to believe him but then, his wife got pregnant and he broke it off.

"Ivory was angry and stalked me for months," said Bakersfield. "She even came here once. She had a hard side to her. I'm not embarrassed to say I was scared of what she might do."

"So then what happened?"

"Nothing. Ivory just went away, stopped calling. But she did send me a text one day. I don't even know how she got my new cell number."

"What did her text say?" I asked.

"All it said was 'You've been replaced.'"

I didn't like this guy. Not only was he a bastard and generally dishonest, he was arrogant. I wanted to call his wife and bust him out and watch her slit his throat but that's not how it goes in the real world. Men still had a code. And besides, I reasoned, these guys always got theirs in the end.

"Is there anything else you can think of that might help me?" I said this with as much sincerity as I could muster.

Before he answered, I knew he was lying because this guy, while slippery, was an amateur. He had tells all over him. He looked down then quickly back up at me.

"No," he said.

I took in a deep breath. Now, I was angry and I didn't mind showing it. I'd been reading some of the most clever assholes in the city from the politicians, to the dirtbag dealers to the best liars of all, the drug addicts and I never appreciated it when an amateur liar tried to put one over on me.

"There's a lot of really bad shit I could say right now," I said, "but it's been a hard day for me already and I don't have the strength. So, just tell me what it is because I know you just lied to me."

"It's kinda personal," said Bakersfield.

"You got no privacy rights here," I said. "Tell it."

"Ivory liked it rough when we did it," he said a little embarrassed. "She liked to be choked and pushed, hair pulled you know, and she liked rough talk too, liked me to say I was gonna hurt her, things like that. I wasn't really into that and she'd make fun of me about it. The girl had a dark side. That's all I'm saying."

I was cool but I have to say that shocked me some. Ivory was vain and mean but never did I think she was a freak.

"Okay doc," I said. "I'm leaving my card. If you think of anything else, contact me and do not tell the press or anyone we talked."

"Believe me, I won't," said Bakersfield.

"And if in the course of my investigation, I find you lied to me about anything, I will break the man code and rain holy shit down on your whole life. Have a good one."

Bakersfield nodded and took my card. I got up, walked to the door but there was one other thing I needed to know.

"Your baby when was it born?"

"Earlier this year," said Bakersfield.

"What did you have?"

"A boy. Name's Eli."

"I got a boy, too, almost a year old. I ain't one to lecture, but you may want to start thinking about the shit you do. It all passes on to our kids, you know."

I left the medical center and I had a bad feeling in my gut about Ivory and her hidden life.

Winter was indeed coming.

PART ONE: LIFE CITY

4

BLUE WATER

I arrived downtown some time later and I was dreading it. My first stop before IAD was my new boss and old partner, Erik Brown, now Captain of the Special Crimes Unit, or the Sewer as we called it.

We were still housed downtown at Police Headquarters on 1300 Beaubien. It was a shit hole that I called home and the only place I ever wanted to work.

It was a bitch getting in as the Black Lives Matter people had staged a pretty big protest rally outside the precinct. I avoided them. I don't think I'm the kind of guy who would be their favorite son.

When I got to The Sewer, all of the guys there expressed their condolences to me and I appreciated that. I could not ask any of them for help because when it came to cops, even dirty ones, we were all blue water, silent and deep. In my heart, I wanted them all to be with me and if any of them knew anything, I trusted they'd find a way to let me know.

On TV, cops work in these offices that look all shiny and new. I only wish we had digs like that. Our place was filled with ancient furniture and even worse equipment. The bankruptcy had tightened our already tight belts and even a special unit like ours was not exempt.

Captain Erik Brown was a great cop and had been promoted for his years of service. He'd shocked me when he revealed that he had hit his wife which led to a divorce after many years.

He seemed much happier these days as he had been dating a lot and was not secretive about how much he was enjoying it.

Erik was a dark-skinned, unassuming man who now sported a mustache and was dressing noticeably better. I didn't dare mention this as Erik was a little sensitive about the money he now had to share with his ex. I was on a mission to gain his favor right now.

"Knew I'd be seeing you," said Erik. "Come on in, partner."

I walked in his office and closed the door. Calling me partner made me know he was on my side even before he said:

"I can't do it and you know I can't."

"Just needed to ask," I said. "You can imagine what I'm up against at home."

"You are an active duty cop, Danny. If you want a temporary transfer to IAD, that will take at least a month and will probably be refused."

"I know. I don't want that. I need you to let the guys and the department know that I asked but was turned down."

Erik looked a little confused and then his brow furrowed and he took on a look I'd seen many times, the bullshit detection look.

"Okay, what the fuck are you up to, Danny?" asked Erik. "Not like you to give up without a fight."

"I got a new case, the murder of a drug dealer. I'm gonna work that case. It might take a while."

Erik smiled a little. "Yes, you do that, in fact, I insist that you get your ass back to work, you may even have to do weekends. I'll sign off on the overtime. You won't get it, but I'll sign."

This is why I loved Erik. He was not the kind of guy who got power and then forgot that he had been a cop. He wanted me on Ivory's murder and if I was working a case, it would allow me to be absent and as long as I sent in progress reports, I'd be fine. I had refused to take a partner after he was promoted and so I was good to go.

"The FBI is grandstanding but they ain't gonna do shit," said Erik. "They don't want no parts of this case. You saw that circus outside."

"Yes, I did. Thanks again, boss."

"Cut that boss shit," said Erik. "Hey, I met a new one, kinda young but promising. She's in grad school and fine as hell."

He whipped out his cell phone and showed me a picture of a young black girl with the biggest ass I'd see in a while.

"Damn," I said not exaggerating. "That real?"

"Damned shame you have to ask that these days. Yes, that's all *au naturale*. What are they feeding these girls?"

"Don't know," I said taking another look.

"How's the boy?" asked Erik.

"He's great. Don't know what's going on. He's lucky."

"And Vinny?"

"Taking it pretty hard."

"I know you and her are going to be poking around," said Erik. "Rumors are flying about who's gonna be a suspect. I don't have to tell you that whoever did this shit is desperate and will kill again if they have to."

"Not if I get them first," I said.

"No cowboy shit," said Erik. "You're somebody's father now."

"You don't have to remind me," I said. "It's taken some of my edge but I'm still good."

"Hey, I saw the picture of the victim," said Erik. "She was a real stunner. You know what that means, right?"

I did. Erik was still a good partner and he couldn't help but to go back into that mode with me. He was always good for reminding me of the angles. Good looking women always went for a certain type of man.

"There are already a few men that fit the bill, " I said. "Talked to one this morning."

"Okay," said Erik. "Go get to your murder case and make sure you cover your ass."

I said goodbye and walked out looking upset and disappointed to cover my ass. I sat at my desk for an hour and then I set out for IAD.

The Internal Affairs Division is at 65 Cadillac Square, not far from The Sewer. No one wanted them in the precinct for fear of surveillance. At least, that's what we said. We just didn't like them much.

Ivory's murder was like Christmas for IAD. It was proof that corruption was real and justified everything they thought of themselves, the guardians of the guardians and all that shit. I know they are necessary but I don't have to like it. Also, I know they got a big ass file on me but I ain't sweatin' it.

I found DeAngela Gomez waiting for me and when I say that, I mean she was looking forward to this, knowing that I'd be in sooner or later.

DeAngela had been a uniformed cop for only two years before going into IAD. It was no secret that she had political ambitions and was currently in a night public policy program at Wayne State. She had future congresswoman written all over her.

She was great looking and had a mane of lustrous dark hair, which she was fond of telling people was one hundred percent real. She also had eyes the same color as mine, rare for a black Latino to have green eyes.

I thought our offices were shitty. The IAD offices where small, cramped and the furniture looked like it was made from matchsticks. But on her desk was a state of the art computer system, a gift from the state probably.

DeAngela was wearing a navy pencil skirt that was as tight as it could be and a top which opened wide to let you have a nice look.

Her hair was down and it cascaded over her shoulders and onto her breasts which were on full display.

"Danny, I am so sorry for your loss," she said and came to me and gave me a hug.

"Thanks," I said knowing she didn't mean it. "You know why I am here, DeAngela."

"And you know I can't share an investigation with an active duty cop, especially one with a dog in the fight. Too risky." She walked to her desk and sat on the edge, a move which made the already tight dress even tighter.

"How bad is it?" I asked. "You can tell me that, at least."

"As bad as you can imagine. Something's rotten in that precinct and everyone has gone brain dead or has amnesia. That girl didn't beam herself into a cell and do herself in. A cop or cops brought her in and they murdered her. And the surveillance tape has gaps in it. Computer malfunction they are saying."

"Bullshit," I said.

"FBI wants to arrest every cop in the precinct or at least the main ones on duty but none of them have any connection to the victim— yet. We have surveillance on all of them, but I don't think any of them will run."

"How many suspects are we talking?" I asked.

"Eight to ten," said DeAngela.

"What about Ivory's friends?" I asked. "She didn't have her phone. But we know who they are from her social media."

"We've gotten to all of them but one, and so far, all we know is she was going to meet some of them downtown but never made it."

"Which one can't we find?" I asked.

"A guy named Raymond Ranier," said DeAngela. "He was the one who invited her. They call him RaRa."

"Is he running?" I asked.

"We don't know."

"Then you need my help," I said.

"Sorry Danny, I want to but—"

"DeAngela, we can play this game if you want but you know you're going to help me. You just need a way that covers your ass. You know the cops are going to go cold on you but I can get info that you can't. Help me and I promise you'll get credit for whatever I find."

She got up from the desk and looked off, assessing. She was probably thinking about what it would mean to her career to close a national case like this. Newspapers, television, talk shows, and all of that sleazy "crime analyst" shit they did these days. It was all good and there was money in it, too.

Then DeAngela walked over to me and she had that look on her face, the one a woman gets when she is about to move outside of the game men and women play around their attraction.

"What if I want more than credit," she said and I could see the seriousness in her eyes.

"What's so special about my dick that you always have to go there?" I asked with as little emotion as I could muster. Always best to go right at it with aggressive women.

"I like that you have integrity and breaking it is part of the thrill. I give it to you and you're mine. Also, I just want it."

"Ain't it dangerous for a politician to be a freak like this?" I asked with just a little smile.

"Only if I fuck a loudmouth. I can't see you being that kind of guy," she said.

"A girl is dead, you know," I said. "That make a difference to you?"

"I am very sorry but you and I know she probably had it coming, Danny. So far, my take on this girl was she was what my mama called a fast girl. Pretty, angry and into manipulating men. Girls like that always get into trouble and you know it."

This really pissed me off but I was close to getting what I wanted and I wasn't going to let my Irish defeat me. And sadly, she was right about Ivory.

"I'm sorry that your heart is so cold but all I'm putting on the table is closing a case that will make your career."

"You really like that girl, huh?"

"If you mean Vinny, the mother of my son, yes."

"I remember you beat some guy all to hell for shooting her," said DeAngela. "I want a man who will do that for me."

"You gotta be a woman that deserves it," I said not missing a beat.

"If you were a real black man, you wouldn't be able to resist this," said DeAngela taking a step back. "The brothers love me."

"I know. I hear them talking all the time but I'm not intrigued by how little blackness a woman has in her. The opposite is what gets to me."

"Wait," said DeAngela smiling. "Are you saying I'm not dark enough?"

"Not *black* enough," I said. "Two different things."

She laughed fully now. "Well, it's nice to know that you just don't like me. I guess I can live with that."

"I never said that," I said. "I like you just fine but you can't have everything you want, no matter how good it looks. A man ain't no good to nobody if he's easily tempted by all the ass life has to offer."

"This is really turning me on," said DeAngela.

"I know," I said with a little triumph in my voice.

She moved away and sat down behind her cheap desk. I fully expected to hear that dress rip as she did but it didn't.

"I'm gonna need a report every couple of days or so and needless to say, you cannot tell anyone. Also, if you make an arrest, I want to be there."

"That could be dangerous," I said. "I can't guarantee that."

"No deal then," said DeAngela. "I'm going to be wherever the action is on this one."

"Okay," I relented, "but if you get shot, I'm gonna have to beat up somebody again."

That got me a big, pretty smile from her. "I'll send you what I have discreetly and it is not to be shared," said DeAngela.

"The first thing I need is a big one," I said. "I need access to the M.E."

****

Dr. Fiona Walker was in very good spirits for a woman who saw death almost every day of her life. Fiona was an albino and had recently gotten contact lenses that gave her normal looking eyes but with her pallid skin, she still disappeared into her white lab coat as she worked.

I stood with her in the cold room over Ivory's body and for once, I was unsettled. It was hard looking at the corpse of someone you knew, especially when she's naked.

I'd called Vinny and told her that I was in. She was elated and did not ask about DeAngela, thankfully.

Vinny sent a list of Ivory's friends back to me. Her cell phone wasn't going to be found and I'd might need to track them down after Fiona gave me the medical info.

"You sure you can handle this, Danny?" asked Fiona.

"Don't have a choice," I said.

"Not surprised to see you. I knew you wouldn't be able to let this go. I'd advise against it but who listens to me."

"I do," I said honestly. "Just not in this case."

"It's not good news," said Fiona. "She was beaten and strangled. See the marks on her face above the ligature. He was probably right handed and… she may have been assaulted sexually before."

"Jesus," I said. And immediately imagined having to tell this to Vinny and the rest of her family.

"I got trauma in the vaginal and anal regions. Whoever did it sanitized the area. I checked for hair and skin. Nothing."

"Or she took a shower," I said. "Could this have just been rough sex?" I asked remembering what Bakersfield had told me.

"Maybe," said Fiona. "The assault happened before the strangulation and get this, I am not certain any of this happened in the precinct. The time of death is very close. So, she could have been killed, then brought in this way."

What happened next is something I cannot fully explain. From somewhere in my knowledge of crime and of Ivory, I began to put things together. The sexual nature of the act had set my mind off. Who would rape a girl and then kill her in a police station or worse do it and then *place* her there? Ivory was indeed a fast girl and very sexually provocative and violent criminals sometimes punished their victim in a way connected to the perceived offense against them.

"Was she pregnant?" I asked.

"How the fuck do you do that?" asked Fiona. "That's goddamned scary, man. Yes, she was just about six weeks, I think."

"Can we determine who the father was if we get a suspect?"

"Yes," said Fiona still looking at me funny. "Anyway, we got nothing from her apartment, just her prints. We might get lucky when we find the car."

"I wouldn't hold my breath on that," I said. "A cop would know just how to get rid of the ride."

I fell silent as Fiona got back into it. I was working out how it could have gone down. Ivory gets stopped and has sex with a rogue cop. They fight, he kills her but why take her to the precinct? No. The cop that got her pregnant, takes her in to talk or to scare her because she won't get rid of the baby and things go left. Maybe.

And who cut the surveillance and how did they get her in and into a cell that's probably controlled by an electric lock? That would be least three men involved...

"I got a boyfriend," said Fiona.

"What?" I asked returning from my thoughts.

"Man, you're a dummy. You can pull that pregnancy shit out of thin air but can't see right before your eyes. Look at me."

I did. Fiona had styled her hair which was almost never done and she was wearing a very nice dress under her boxy lab coat.

"I uh, congratulations. I'm sorry."

"It's okay. I know you got a lot to think about. This is the first man who's been interested in me since I started getting treated for my albinism. I'm never gonna be nice and pink like the other girls, but I'm not suffering any of the other symptoms anymore."

"That's great, Fiona," I said a little hesitantly. Fiona was a friend and one of the best ME's in the nation. She was always there to help me and yet I had never thought of her as an actual person. She struggled with her affliction and was working hard to become whole again and I had not even noticed. "I'm sorry, I've been distracted with stuff."

"I know, a baby, promotion, new house, a free one."

"Well, it was. They reneged on that and so now we do have to pay for it, but we got a good price."

"I'm not mad," said Fiona. "I'm happy for you. God knows you need some happiness. If it wasn't for Vinny, I'm pretty sure you'd be dead by now... or a lot of bad guys would be. Anyway, I hate to do this to you but I want you to meet my guy. You got a good sense of people and before I go too far with him, I want you to give him the once over."

"Sure, I will Fiona," I said. "I guess we're all kinda broken in this business."

"How's the baby?"

"Great," I said.

"Must be," she said. "You look like you want to smile but can't. That's real progress."

She looked at me for a moment, and her eyes fluttered over the contacts she wore which hid the ice gray of her real eyes and I noticed for the first time that despite her very pale skin, that she was a nice looking woman. Suddenly, I felt guilty, like I'd been neglecting her all these years.

"Be careful telling your family about this," said Fiona. "It won't make things better."

"I don't want to tell them," I said. "Not until we get a suspect in custody."

Fiona wrapped it up for me and it was clear that Ivory had died a very nasty and violent death. A man had killed a woman and her unborn baby, a baby that was his.

I thought briefly about my son and what it would take for me to harm a child. Whoever my killer was, he had no heart, which made him a much more dangerous man than me.

5

RENARDO

For so long, he had been something else, a criminal they said, a lowlife scum and the like. But that was only because drugs were still a dirty business to most folks. Silly, but that's how it was.

What were people going to hate when drugs became legal, he wondered? It was just a matter of time. Look at Colorado and Oregon. They almost got it in Ohio, but they got greedy. Funny how white men were going to make money off something they used to lock up black men, by making it a business.

Well, now he was a businessman, shady maybe but he wore a suit and tie and did not have to look over his shoulder each day.

Renardo Peoples had done his time in the crews, selling whatever shit ass package the big boys dropped on the street. He saw all his friends die or go to jail and watched as the so-called legends went down one by one: T-Bone, The Union, Gregory Cane and last year, iDT.

But he had survived because he was smart. He followed the rules. He never used drugs. He only hooked up with good girls and did not get them pregnant. He bought off the violent cops but never told them anything. He saved his money and most of all, he never killed unless he absolutely had to. Now, he would fuck your ass up, but killing? People still got all bent out of shape about that, as if they really cared about any of these people in the 'hood.

Dope was a good business no matter what people said but it was going out of style. Getting high was slowly being accepted by America. We had at least three Presidents who admitted getting high. So, it was just a matter of time before everybody understood that getting high was a fact of life. And then what? They'd be selling crack in the grocery store right next to the broccoli.

Renardo saw a better business in Detroit now and he had seen it way before the city went down in that damned bankruptcy.

Real estate.

Soon, the white folks would come back into the city to take what was theirs and they would push all the blacks out to the suburbs and into pockets of shitty neighborhoods. And he was ready for it. He knew which neighborhoods white folks would covet and so for the last three years, he had been forcing these old ass bible thumping grannies out.

He'd wait until they got into trouble or one of their worthless ass kids, then he'd move in with cold, hard cash for the house. They went for it and then he'd low-ball them. From there he and his partner would sell high or hold on to it depending on where it was.

He sat across from one such granny now, a woman who had agreed to sell to him and then changed her mind, after taking the advance, of course. She had the money on the table and was giving it back to him.

Renardo was an odd-looking man. He was lanky with a long face and a beard that he kept groomed along with his afro. He had long arms and long fingers on which he wore rings of different colors, like his man The Mandarin. He favored dark sun glasses even indoors because he felt it made him look menacing. Once, he was mistaken for the rap artist, André 3000.

Renardo had tried every manner of reason with this granny but she had it in her head that her minister was right and that she should get out of the deal she made with no contract. Contracts were messy and so Renardo stayed away from them until the end.

"Miss Temple," said Renardo. "We had a deal and I kept it off the books so you could use the advance to get your grandson out of trouble. He's out now, right?"

The grandson in question, a fat, simple-faced boy named Bramah sat next to his granny and looked as guilty and upset as you might imagine. He kept his eyes averted, knowing that all of this was his fault.

"Yes," said Miss Temple. "And I thank you for that, it was a blessing, but my pastor, the Reverend Paymer says my house is worth a lot more than you're giving me."

She was a nice looking lady of about sixty-five. She had long black and gray hair that she pressed and tied back. She looked considerably younger which most black women did. And Miss Temple had a beautiful set of false teeth, which had been a present from her daughter on her last birthday.

"It might be worth more but it might not be," said Renardo. "I'm taking that risk. None of that is relevant because you made a promise to me and now you're taking it back."

"And I feel bad about that," said Miss Temple. "I know what I said but I was desperate and now I see things clearly."

"Where'd you get this money on the table?" asked Renardo.

"My pastor gave it to me," said Miss Temple.

"I see," said Renardo. He took the money from the table and stuffed it into his jacket pocket.

"Thank you for being so understanding," said Miss Temple. "I didn't want any trouble. You see, Bramah," she said to her grandson. "I told you he'd understand. People are all reasonable in the Lord's House."

"I'm disappointed," said Renardo. "And so I'm sorry for what I have to do."

"What?" said Miss Temple.

"I have to take action for this slight and the lie you told me. It's nothing personal."

"What you gonna do?" said Miss. Temple, her voice rising. "I got people to protect me in case you thinking about hurting me and I got Jesus. I fear no man and no instrument formed against me shall—"

"Yeah, I know," said Renardo standing up. "I know all that shit Reverend Payment says in church and I know why he gave you that cash. He is going to get a piece of what you will get for selling this house, right?"

"That's none of your business," said Miss Temple straightening her back. "And his name is Paymer, not *payment.* I know what people call him behind his back but you respect him in this house."

"You notice he's not here right now, standing behind his investment," said Renardo. "And do you know why? Because Payment knows I got to take action against someone for this deal going bad. And he knows it ain't gonna be you. I'd never hurt an old lady. Bad for business. But your grandson here might get hit by a car on his way to the store one night, or he might just not come back home at all and then you won't even be able to collect the insurance I know you got on him. And you got his mama, Camelia, who lives three streets over and got them other four grandbabies by the three different brothers. Girl can't keep them legs closed, can she?"

"I think you need to leave my house, young man," said Miss Temple. "Now."

"Did you know that just last week, a little girl was found in an alley, beat up, violated and pumped full of drugs," said Renardo. "There's a lot of perverts 'round here would pay cash money for a young girl. Two of them grandkids is girls, ain't they?"

Miss Temple's eyes were so wide, it looked like they would just roll out of her head.

"You get out of my house, devil!" her voice cracked. "Bramah, throw him out!"

Renardo looked at the grandson and now Renardo's face was no longer neutral; he had a look that Bramah had seen many times. You see, in the 'hood, a lot of shit is very nonverbal, you get a sense of danger and just how far you can go. Deals made with the devil cannot be rescinded on a whim. They are always paid in flesh.

"We need to keep the deal," said Bramah quietly.

"What?" said Miss Temple. "Boy, are you out of your feeble mind?"

"No grandma," said Bramah. "I'm sorry I caught that case and put you in this situation but Renardo is right, you don't do this to people round here… not to him."

"He don't scare me," said Miss Temple.

"*You* ain't supposed to be," said Bramah a little too loudly. "Listen to the man."

Miss Temple looked at her grandson and though he was a dimwitted boy, he was not one to lie or exaggerate.

Then she looked to Renardo and finally saw it. He would kill her family and think nothing of it. He had probably done it many times and now he was here in her house. Death. And she had let him in. Satan was indeed a beautiful Angel who never hid, but fooled you with his normalcy. It had been right in front of her and she just didn't want to see it. She should have let this dumbass boy go to jail.

Renardo took out the money and some papers and held them out. Miss Temple took them with shaking hands and signed the contract, all the while cursing.

"This ain't right," said Miss Temple.

"Thank you," said Renardo, taking the quitclaim deed and other papers. "I will bring your money tomorrow by cashier's check. And like we agreed, there will be a cash amount. You will have two months to live here without any rent but then you have to go."

"God's gonna get you," said Miss Temple.

"Not really," said Renardo. "I'll ask for forgiveness and he'll forgive me. It's a really good deal, this Jesus thing." Renardo got up, turned and walked to the door.

"Get the hell out of my house!" said Miss Temple. "Lowlife sonofabitch!"

Renardo stopped and Bramah jumped up, almost knocking over his chair and jumping in front of his granny. He was about to say something, when Renardo held out a hand, silencing him.

"I could be upset at you for talking to me that way," said Renardo, "but I know you're used to it. The men these days are so full of bitchassness that women have forgotten those old rules, the old time, when if you talked against a man, he'd slap the shit out of you. Your worthless grandson here and the man who obviously left your ass years ago, all bitches."

Renardo picked some lint off his suit and flicked it into the air where it drifted up and away.

Bramah was about to piss his pants. He waited for Renardo to reach into his jacket, pull out a gun and then shoot him. He'd hit him in the leg or the arm, something that wouldn't kill him but would hurt like hell. Or, he'd pull out one of them nightsticks and hit his granny over the head and stomp her until he broke something. But he didn't. Renardo brushed off his sleeve and looked back at the old woman.

"See, I believe in that," Renardo continued. "I believe that women need to be kept in check by reminding them that God made us bigger and stronger to protect, to kill food for the table and to fuck you up when you forget your goddamned place in the order of things. All these ladies in the 'hood now walk around like they got dicks between their legs. That's why none of y'all can keep a man past Thursday. See, a man would have gotten the money you needed some other way. He would not have sold his home and then tried to slide out of it, but you're not a man, you're an old woman who was used to trading on her ass for everything. Well, nobody in life gives a shit about you anymore. So, the next time you see me, you talk with respect or I will go back on my old lady policy and I will be the last thing you see before you go to meet Jesus."

Renardo waited a second, knowing that they both would be terrified that he would be moved to violence. In truth, Renardo did not have a weapon on him but they didn't know that.

He turned and left, walked outside and got into his car, a black GMC that was driven by his man, Kelvin, an ex-con who was on probation for distribution.

"She do it?" asked Kelvin.

"Why you ask a dumbass question like that?" asked Renardo settling in.

"Sorry."

"I had to give her the God made men speech."

"I love that speech. It's Sam Jackson cold," said Kelvin.

"He only wishes he was as cold as me," said Renardo. "And his name is Samuel. Man don't like to be called Sam. Got half a mind to go back in there and smack them store bought teeth out of that old bitch but you know I'm trying to change and shit."

"You doin' good, boss," said Kelvin. "You ain't fucked up niggas nearly as much this year as you did last year. Last year was like whoo!"

"I'm a businessman," said Renardo, as if reminding himself. "A CEO don't shoot muthafuckas if the profits is down. I know they want to, but they're civilized. So, how many more we got today?"

"Two more," said Kelvin. "Mr. Wilson already signed and we just need to pick up his papers."

"I like that old dude. I'ma give him a little bonus for being so cool."

"Well, don't get happy yet. The Melvins still say no. They the only ones on that block not to sell. Rev. Payment got to them, too."

"I need that whole block to complete that patch," said Renardo sounding frustrated. "They the ones with the kids that live in Texas."

"Yeah," said Kelvin. "They ain't got no, what you call it?"

"Vulnerabilities," said Renardo. "When a man's got vulnerabilities you can make him do anything. I'll worry about them later. Let's go."

****

Kelvin hopped on the freeway and drove out of the city. The sky was looking angry and he hoped it didn't rain. That shit would freeze and you'd be driving on ice. He hated that.

They traveled on M-14 headed toward Ann Arbor. They stopped in a little city called Plymouth and pulled into a breakfast place that specialized in waffles. In the back, sitting at his usual table, was the man Renardo was looking for.

He didn't like coming to meet him. Man always wanted to go way outside the city for some reason and Renardo hated the way suburban white folks looked at him, like some animal got out of its cage.

"I don't get it," said Renardo sitting down across from the man. "You live in Grosse Pointe but you never like to see me in the city."

"I got my reasons," said the man whose name was Thom Ross. "This place has no security cameras and they don't allow any cell phones or computers. You can talk here."

Thom was forty-five or so and had at one point been the CEO of a tech firm. He'd bought some small companies and sold them for big money. Unfortunately, he bet big on the tech market and didn't get out before the bubble burst.

He lost everything and got a job working for a data services company owned by the Bell family, one of the state's richest clans. He had hit the jackpot and married their daughter. There was new money, old money and Bell money. Their Ancestors went all the way back to Detroit's trading post days.

Thom finally found a woman worthy of his lost greatness when he met Sandra Bell. She was a rather plain girl and he was the handsome but poor employee who had crapped out of the big time. They were married within a year.

Thom was now one of the biggest property owners in Detroit. He had been buying up lots and depressed houses in the 'hood since 2008 and had accumulated quite a big tract of land. Thom was a visionary, just like Renardo.

He'd found Renardo by accident when the two of them were trying to get the same property. They joined forces and so far it had been very lucrative.

Thom had told Renardo that he was making moves in real estate because his wife's family kept a tight hold on the money. He was looking to get his own funds and get out.

Renardo had agreed because it was a good deal and also, Thom was a player. He acted refined but underneath, he was a hard man who would get his no matter what. You had to respect that.

"You really wear fucking sunglasses in the winter?" asked Thom.

"Cool has no seasons," said Renardo.

"How'd you do today?" asked Thom.

"Good," said Renardo. "I got a problem on that block by Van Dyke but I'll figure it out."

"We need that block," said Thom.

"Don't worry," said Renardo.

"But I do worry because it represents a significant investment and upside. I've been entrusted to deliver it all intact."

"I know all that, man. Just let me handle it."

"Listen, I wanted to see you because things have changed a little. After we secure that block, we should settle up and close out."

"What?" said Renardo. "We ain't near where we want to be yet."

"Again, that's why I wanted to meet in person," said Thom. "The plan has changed for me and I don't like delivering bad news on the phone."

"Changed? How?" asked Renardo his voice rising. "Don't be fucking with me, man."

"I needed to do this real estate thing before," said Thom. "I was in a cash bind and this was my way out but now, I'm good. I can trade my real estate position to some big buyers and cash out. But don't worry, I'm gonna take care of you. I can give you what we agreed to plus ten percent."

"What we agreed to was that I'd be a millionaire," said Renardo removing his sunglasses. "You said we'd build a company and run property management together. Black and white kings, remember that shit?"

"Like I said, things have changed for me. I am offering you the cash equivalent of the shares I promised plus a ten percent bump. You should be dancing."

Renardo began to laugh softly, then louder. "I see. You fuckin' me. It's all nice and business-like, but this is an ass rape with no muthafuckin' Vaseline."

"You're pulling three times out of this what you put in," said Thom. "How is that screwing you over? Plus, you made a friend who can bring you into any legit deal I come across from now on. Win-win."

"It ain't what I did this for. Everything is in your name because of my record. All I had was trust and you're using that against me now."

"Renardo, you have got to learn to see the bigger picture," said Thom. "That's why I'm in business with you because you're not like those dumbasses in Detroit."

"You mean other niggas," said Renardo.

"Yes, that's exactly what I mean," said Thom. "Don't try to intimidate me with that word. You are not a nigger and that's why I like you. But you have got to think outside the box more."

"You drag me out here to whitey land and then drop this on me thinking I'm not gonna act out because I'm in Plymouth. Fuck Plymouth. You don't know who you talking to."

"So what you gonna do? Threaten me? Resort to violence? Go on. Let's see who wins that one. You may not be a nigger but you are still black."

"Okay," said Renardo. "Instead of resorting to gangsta shit, let's just call it twenty-five percent over my payout and we can be done." He put the sunglasses back on.

Suddenly, Thom laughed and clapped his hands together.

"You, are good, my friend," said Thom. "You have really learned from me, haven't you? Okay, so we're negotiating now."

"You got things to lose, too," said Renardo. "Don't think your fancy partners would like to come to a meeting and meet me and maybe hear about how we do what we do in the city."

"Twelve percent," said Thom.

"Twenty."

"Fifteen."

"Seventeen."

"Done," said Thom. "Now see, that's business. I can have your money by the end of next month. Just bring me those last few properties, including the Van Dyke tract and we're good."

"We're gonna split fifty-fifty on anything now, including today's business," said Renardo.

"No way," said Thom. "Same deal, same split."

"Then, you go into the city and talk some old black folks out of their home," said Renardo. "I'm sure they will welcome you."

Renardo leaned back confidently in his chair. Thom stewed but knew when he was beaten.

"Fine, fifty-fifty," said Thom. "Now who's getting screwed?"

"Stop crying," said Renardo. "Just have my money ready on time."

Renardo got up and walked out of the restaurant. He looked cool but his mind was already working out a plan of action and behind his dark glasses, his eyes raged with cold anger.

6

INFO

The sun was going down around five or so when I got home, it was dark out. The news crews were gone and I was happy to see my street free from those vultures.

I used to admire reporters when I was a kid. They were kinda like information cops. They didn't carry guns, but that microphone and the camera could do just as much damage.

Now, they all seemed like liars, opportunists and whores. They don't seem interested in the news or even in facts. Perhaps we have all become too cynical or maybe we finally see them for what they have always been.

I got out of my car. A light snow had been falling for over an hour and it had settled on everything. That first light blanket of snow told you not to get your hopes up until April.

I lived in a section of the city called Rosedale Park in an area now called the Blue Mile because so many cops lived there. The city had given us free houses and then quickly reneged on the deal when they filed bankruptcy.

I walked toward my house, when I saw my next door neighbor's front door fling open. He had been waiting for me, watching all day, I bet. I took in a deep breath, preparing myself.

"Danny!" said the man named Lenny Johnston. He was white, about forty or so and worked for the city in some obscure department with "Planning" in the title. He was married to a black woman, which he felt made us kindred spirit. He padded out to me, wearing a robe and slippers.

"Long day, Lenny," I said trying to convey a message that I did not want to be pestered.

"I know and my condolences but I wanted to talk to you, about the case," said Lenny.

"There is no case," I said, "and if there was, I could not talk with you about it."

"I got some theories," said Lenny, ignoring me. "I know the IAD is probably snooping around but they won't find anything, code of silence and all."

Lenny was an amateur detective. He loved those TV shows where they find killers in thirty minutes and the movies, where the police leveled a city block to catch one bad guy.

"I'm tired Lenny and we are in mourning. I can't talk."

"Okay," said Lenny. "Just one thing. The cell phone. The killer is probably on the dead girl's cell. If you get it—"

"Her name is Ivory and I am sure the police are on it. Now, I gotta go. It's cold as hell out here."

"Man, I'm never going to get used to hearing that voice come out of your face."

"Lenny, come back in. Hi Danny," said Lenny's wife Stephanie. She was considerably younger than Lenny, still in her late twenties and had two kids that were not Lenny's. Not a bad deal for her, I thought. Lenny was a pest but he was loyal. No price tag on that.

"Okay, just talking shop," said Lenny. To me, he said: "Think about it and let me know."

He walked back to the house and I saw Stephanie give me a sympathetic look. I nodded my head, then headed into the house.

Vinny was waiting for me when I got inside. RMC was crawling around trying to stand up.

"He's still trying," I said. "He's gonna make it soon."

Vinny kissed me as I took off my coat and hat and shoes by the door. She'd been very affectionate since the death and I was not complaining about it. I knew she was worried about me.

"That Lenny out there?" she asked.

"Yes. He's solved the case already."

I went into the kitchen and soon I was holding RMC as I ate my dinner. I fed him a little. Boy couldn't stand to see other people eat without him.

"So, did you get anything?" asked Vinny.

"Yes," I said and I told her everything I knew except that her sister was a freak. No need to go there yet.

"Damn," said Vinny. "A married doctor. Ivory was never one to shrink away from controversy or a dick."

I laughed a little at her joke and she smiled, realizing that she had made one.

"So you know what I'm thinking," I said. "A bad cop or maybe two did this and covered it up because of the baby."

"Then all we need are suspects and a DNA match," said Vinny.

"Yeah but we gotta get 'em first. I heard there are going to be maybe ten suspects in all."

"What about the doctor?" asked Vinny. "He could be the father."

"I'll get a sample from him," I said. "But I don't think he's the father. I know this sounds crazy, but if he was, he'd own up to it."

"Thank God I wasn't there with you. I might have stomped his ass," said Vinny.

"I thought about it," I said. "But as Mr. El said, you know Ivory."

"What did he mean by that?" asked Vinny.

When you lose someone, I think your brain just wipes out all reason and logic about the dead person. All you remember are the good things and compromises on the bad. But we were trying to find a murderer and there was no reason to soft peddle the victim to another cop.

"He meant Ivory was hard-headed, mean and arrogant," I said. "She was playing men and she messed with the wrong guy."

This hurt Vinny's feelings a little but I could see her processing this truth.

"We were trying to get her to change," said Vinny. "Me, Easter, Ivanna, all of us. But she was just so full of herself. She put up a picture on Instagram of herself coming out of the shower and it got a hundred thousand likes. That's like a whole damned city worth of men. We couldn't compete with that."

"Erik used to say, 'ain't no cure for young and pretty,'" I said. "Think I know what he meant now."

"Another thing," said Vinny. "We found money at Ivory's place, a lot of it."

"How much?" I asked.

"Six thousand and change. Cash," said Vinny.

Now my head was filled with thoughts of drug deals and payoffs. No way Ivory earned that kind of jack at her job.

"That's not good," I said. "Anything else there?"

"No," said Vinny. "We're gonna use the money to bury her."

The baby began to cry and I resisted the impulse to pass him to his mother. I'd done that a lot and had gotten told off about it.

Vinny reached for the baby and I passed him over. I guess she was feeling very maternal given recent events.

"IAD's gonna have those suspects soon," I said. "As soon as tomorrow, I'm hoping."

"Man, we sure are taking a beating lately," said Vinny. "Don't know what's gotten into folks. Shoot first, kill a man if he doesn't want to comply. What the fuck?"

"It's a lot of things," I said. I'd been thinking about this for a while. "First, we gotta stop making it so easy to get on the force. It's not like working in a damned supermarket. You don't get the job if you can lift the gun. Some of these new cops are weak and angry and that's a bad combination. If I could, I'd throw out about twenty percent of the guys."

"And who do we get to replace them? No one wants the job anymore."

"That's the second thing. We need to get paid more money. This volunteer for nobility shit is over. Just like the Army. Make it a good ass job and the best men will come for it."

"Not even," said Vinny laughing a little. "You got your job because of your father in part. We have to get rid of the nepotism and bias in the hiring and I wouldn't hold my breath for that."

"Hold up," I said. "You trying to say I would not have been a cop if it wasn't for my dad?"

"It would have been harder," said Vinny. "And yes, maybe you might not have made it the first time. Didn't you have some psych issues?"

She was right. I did. I didn't do so good on the test and the psychologist flagged me. My father and some other cops vouched for me and it all went away. Damn, I hated it when she was right about racial shit.

"You got me," I said. "But I wouldn't have given up."

"I'm already worried," said Vinny, as her face suddenly went flat. "When RMC gets to be a teenager, what are cops gonna think when they see him?"

This was something I did not want to talk about. Because I was white, I was in some real denial about my son being something else. I wanted him to just be a person, but that was not going to happen. He was definitely a black boy and his lighter skin, hair and eyes would not make a damned bit of difference to some asshole. In fact, I knew that he would likely get shit from black *and* white people and that made me even more upset.

"They're gonna treat him like any other black kid," I said. "Whatever that will be in fifteen years. I just hope I don't have to kill somebody if something happens to him because I don't think anyone could stop me— or you."

Now it was her turn to laugh. Vinny was more even-tempered but she was a lot meaner.

"You get anything in suit land?" I asked looking to change the subject.

"Some," said Vinny. "The city is already dreading a lawsuit and the big shots had a big meeting about the bad publicity now that the city is coming back. Just like I thought, there's talk about cleaning out the 11th. The Black Lives Matter people are getting permits for a rally and they are still calling us but we are not going in with them."

"They could be useful to us down the road," I said.

"How?" she asked.

"They attract a lot of attention and no one will be looking at us, you feel me?"

"I do," said Vinny. "Marcus Jr. and Ivanna have friends in the group. I'll tell them to keep a life-line open with one of them just in case."

I finished my dinner and then Vinny got RMC ready for bed. She read to him each night even though he had no idea what she was saying. This was supposed to make him smarter in the long run.

I took a turn even though I thought it was silly. He did seem to like that book called *Go, Dog. Go!*

Vinny and I called the family and let them know some of the things we knew. We held back the nastier elements for now and assured them that Ivory's body would soon be released.

I planned out my next steps on my cover case as well as who I would talk to next on Ivory's murder. So far, I knew a lot of Ivory's personal business but nothing that could lead me to her killer or killers.

In my heart, I was so glad that we didn't have a girl. I don't think many men want girls because of the world we live in. We treat women like shit and then fear for our own women in the world we've made against them.

Vinny called me to come into the bedroom and I was surprised when she stepped out of the bathroom wearing a full business suit and high heels. Her braids fell over one shoulder and she pushed some of them back over.

"I have court tomorrow," she said. "What do you think?"

"You look good, I mean smart," I joked.

"Too sexy?" she asked as she turned letting me see it all.

Now, I knew this was about DeAngela. See, there are two ways a woman can go if she's feeling jealous or intimidated by another woman. She can chastise you for being a man or she can reward you and make you remember that you already made the only choice you need to make.

Vinny's outfit was too sexy. The skirt was really short and her top plunged down showing as much breast as she could. She looked like a businesswoman in a porno.

"You might want to pull back some," I said as I felt myself getting worked up about it. "I thought you didn't want me to get into how you dress."

"Just asking," she said and this time, she didn't even try to hide her intention. "Here, help me get this off."

Vinny turned her hip to me and patted it by a zipper. I walked over and kissed her as I pushed her into the bathroom and slowly pulled that zipper down. I had to peel that skirt off her it was so tight, but I got it done.

Vinny started to take my shirt off but I stopped her. Instead, I continued to undress her until she was fully naked— except for the shoes, of course.

We kissed some more and she tried to undress me again but I stopped her. I liked her being the one exposed.

I moved in for the kill, then the baby made a noise and immediately we both stopped and waited. This was a new reality of life as a parent. There was another person in the house.

I went to check on RMC. He was fine. When I came back, Vinny was on the bed, still naked, shoes on and waiting.

"Get in here," she said.

I pretty much ripped off my clothes as I was now over the game and eager to get it. One of my buttons flew off my shirt as we tugged at it.

PART ONE: LIFE CITY

We engaged in the familiarities of each other's sexual preferences and it was good as always. Vinny is a full-bodied woman with beautiful skin and a beautiful face. Often, I take small moments to just look at her and savor her loveliness, moments that I know turn her on.

We kissed and licked and grabbed at each other as I kept a steady rhythm and she struggled to keep quiet.

"I love you, so much," she said.

It was unusual for her to be given to this kind of statement during sex but I knew it was the tragedy and the need to feel human in a world that was suddenly filled with inhumanity.

"I love you too," I said, not missing a beat.

It felt good to say this during this connection knowing that the next day, we would both be back to the grim business of finding a killer.

7

CHICKEN BOX

I walked into Regina's Honey Fried Chicken a little after it opened at ten. It was an unassuming little place that was known for having some of the best fried chicken in the city. Rumor was, Regina Long pressure cooked her chicken after dipping it in a batter made of honey and other secret ingredients.

There were only two customers eating at a little table, but the place had a long line for carryout. In that line, I saw the usual working folk, a couple of single moms who were on the dole and a kid who should have been in school, who was probably cutting or maybe working in a crew.

None of them really held my attention as I moved to the head of the line and showed the cashier my badge and asked for the manager, Mr. Long.

In the back, Regina herself worked with her employees. She did not see me and I wasn't here to see her, so I said nothing but I did get a good whiff of what she was cooking and it smelled like heaven.

The chicken joint's neighborhood was also home to a local drug dealer named Every Wadson who had been killed last week. Every. That was one I had never heard.

Black people name their kids what seem to be strange and made up names. People unfamiliar with the culture often laugh, even as they name their kids "Scout" and "Apple" and shit like that.

Well, of course it comes from a place of pain and theft of culture and history. I know this because I've been lectured by friends, colleagues and criminals over the years. Every's mom just wanted her boy to have some uniqueness of his own, something that he could carry with him forever.

Every Wadson and his unique name terrorized the little neighborhood, selling dope, running off rivals and collecting protection from the local businesses. If you didn't pay him, he'd send some young kids to your place and vandalize it at night or maybe deface your ride or worse.

I was sure Regina's had been paying him. Every had most folks afraid of him and rightly so. He was a violent criminal born to a mother who had been one of the most notorious drug dealers in the early 1980's.

Shirley Wadson was called "Ice" on the street because she had the peculiar habit of sucking on ice cubes instead of drinking water. She was killed in a gunfight but not before leaving the world her little bundle of joy.

Someone had had enough of this nigga and killed him, let him have it with his own gun. They'd blown his head off. Shot him in the neck at close range and his head fell to one side, hanging on by a few muscles and skin. The killer had dropped the gun, wiped his prints and took off.

And yes, I do say the N-word, but only to myself. All white people do. Let's just leave it at that.

This was a major crime because the deceased was connected to two major drug suppliers and the savagery of the killing suggested a turf war. I didn't think so, but that idea served my purpose.

Every smoked a lot of weed and had a bad habit of using his own stash and was known to get high and sleep from about noon to three each day, normal down time for drug boys.

Last week, while he was asleep, someone just walked into his house and shot him. Every just sat there in the chair for days until the smell alerted his neighbors.

No one had said anything and no one was talking so far. I had to officially start working this case so I figured I should check out Every's killer and make sure he did not skip town. Yes, I knew who did it. I knew the night I went to the dead drug dealer's house.

"Mr. Long?" I said as a man opened the rear door and walked out.

"Yes," said the man who was about forty-five, black and as mild mannered looking a guy as I'd ever seen.

"I'm Detective Cavanaugh. I'd like a moment of your time."

"What about?" asked John Long nervously. "Not that drug dealer?"

He had a look of alarm in his eyes. I would too, if I had killed a man and a detective came to my door.

"Yes. I'm working the case," I said calmly.

"What do you want from me?" asked John.

"I'm interviewing potential witnesses from the neighborhood. You were there that night when we investigated."

"We were all watching, the whole street," said John looking a little calmer now. "Boy was a menace, in case you didn't know."

"We do know. Can I speak to you in the back office?" I asked.

"Oh yes, sure."

We walked into the office and it was actually a very nice one. It looked like a mini executive suite. I guess John didn't care that his customers had a shitty place to eat but he would be damned of he didn't have a nice office to work in.

"I remember you," said John. "Not many white boys sound like that. Where'd you grow up?"

"East side, outside of Hamtramck," I said.

"*Pączkis*," said John. "Man, I love those. City's full of them damned Arabs now."

"I don't want to take up too much of your time. I'm trying to close the case and I have a theory."

"Okay," said John. "Make it quick because I have to get back to work soon."

"No problem," I said. "I noticed that Every had some of your chicken at his place when he died. He probably liked to get high and eat it. But he was asleep when he was shot, according to the M.E."

"Yeah, he was a regular," said John. "You can see, a lot of people are. We sell a good product."

"But you don't deliver," I said. "Someone brought him that chicken. Don't think he bought it then fell asleep before eating. His meal was untouched. In fact, it was in the garbage. Someone put it in there. They actually picked up some trash to hide the chicken box under it. It didn't take a genius to figure out whoever brought that chicken, also shot the man."

"Maybe one of his crew brought it," said John, too quickly. "They come in for him all the time."

"I thought about that," I said. "Funny thing is, they all have a good alibi. They got picked up by the police for selling around the time of the murder."

John was shaking now and I knew he'd lose it in a second. He walked over to his sofa and sat on the arm.

"I knew it," said John. "I know that—"

"Now, I don't know who did it," I said, cutting him off. "Really, I'd like to give whoever did it a medal. Every Wadson was suspected in at least three murders, convicted of robbery and assault. Once, he was going to prison for raping a thirteen year old girl, when the victim's mother mysteriously broke her arm and then the victim refused to testify. Also, he beat a dog to death a year ago, according to your neighbors."

"He did," said John in a low voice. "It was my neighbor's dog. Roscoe got loose and was barking loudly and… Yes, Every was a bad person, terrible. I didn't mean—"

"You should know," I said, "that I plan to investigate this murder for the next few months. Thing is, I'm just working on a theory here and I'm not sure if this chicken clue will lead anywhere, even though I have what looks to be a good fingerprint on the box that chicken was in."

John winced as I said this. He had been careful not to leave fingerprints on the gun, but he rushed to get out and in his haste, had forgotten that he touched the chicken box. I had not taken the box to forensics. It was in a plastic bag in evidence. I was just holding it but John didn't know that.

"So, be careful what you say," I continued. "It could make me have to do something I don't want to do."

John was much calmer now as he had figured out that I had no intention of taking him in for killing a piece of filth like Every Wadson.

"I uh, okay," said John. "But what do I— uh what would a person do if that chicken box business was real?"

"He would call my boss in three weeks and complain that I am harassing him trying to solve this case and he would get a very trusted friend to do the same for him, three weeks later and he would make sure both complaints were in writing, email form, so that it will go in my reports."

"Okay," said John. "Okay, detective. I got it and I'll mark it on my calendar. Thank you."

"Don't thank me yet," I said. "I will close this case. I just need time to find a way so that no good people get into trouble."

"Yes," said John. "I see."

"Good. You know, someone else will come to replace Every. All you business people here can stop that by banding together. Easier than waiting for someone to do what someone did to Every."

"You're pretty smart to have figured all that out," said John.

"Not really," I said. "Every Wadson was a bad person and sooner or later guys like that get got by someone. Dealers would have either dumped him or just disappeared his ass. I knew it wasn't a pro and since most murders are committed by men, here I am talking to you, instead of your wife. But this is all still theoretical."

"Why do you want me to complain about you then?" asked John.

"Don't think you should be asking questions right now," I said.

He just nodded. It had been quite a day for him and I didn't want to make it any worse. I reminded him not to leave town and said goodbye. I turned to leave, then something important occurred to me.

"Oh, can I get a number two to go?" I asked. "I'm gonna be hungry in a minute."

8

THE BELLS

Thom Ross drove up to the guard house. He saw the old black man wave like always and like always, he ignored him. His wife loved to stop and chat with the help, but it was not his style. He had no guilt about the lower classes. There were reasons people were separated and he believed in them.

He drove into the circular drive of his home in Grosse Pointe Shores. The beauty and serenity of the three story mansion and its wintery backdrop stood in stark contrast to what he was feeling. Inside, he was a raging mixture of emotions but he had to keep it all very low for now.

"These are the times that try men's souls," he said quoting someone he could not remember.

Renardo had unsettled him a little the other day. He was not nearly as smart as he had thought. He was hoping the black man would be happy but just like a lot of his people, he didn't know the difference between money and wealth. Renardo thought just getting money guaranteed him wealth but it does not work that way. Wealth was akin to power and that was built over time. When an opportunity came, you took it, then moved on. Most of his kind had the lottery mentality.

Thom was mad when he left. Renardo had out-negotiated him. The black man would probably try to strike back at him after he got paid, but Thom had a plan for that.

He was going to a place where he could not take a man like Renardo and it had nothing to do with his color, well, it did a little but there were realities to life that we all had to accept. No one knew that as well as he did.

Thom got out of the car as one of the house staff came and took it to be put away. He entered the home and another staffer took his coat and scarf.

"Good evening sir," said Thelma, one of their house workers. She was a maid although he had trouble thinking of her that way.

"Evening, Thelma," said Thom. "Is Mrs. Ross about?"

"Yes, sir," said Thelma, a middle aged woman who wore immaculate wigs each day. Today's wig was jet black and very pleasing, he thought. "She's taking dinner. She didn't want to wait."

As Thom walked toward the small dinning room which was in the east-wing of the house, he made an effort not to look at the walls of family portraits of the Bells.

He knew those pictures very well. They started with Ewan Lukas Belleten, an immigrant from Scotland and his wife, Gerta Steinhaus, a German. They were married, then a quick slash to the name and Belleten became Bell.

They settled in Michigan and became traders and lumber dealers and later invested in gas, oil and a new thing called the automobile. The family became wealthy very quickly and several of the Bells lost vast sums of money through foolishness. That was when Ewan Bell came up with the family trust that has protected them and their money ever since.

In the modern age, the Bell family passed to Quinn Bell, a famously hard man who had built the family fortune with his father and grandfather.

Quinn was a soldier, a hunter and a notorious ladies man, who was rumored to have several mixed race children. He carried on the tradition and built even more wealth in the industrial age of America.

Over the years, the Bells were involved in just about every major event in the nation one way or another. They helped black slaves flee to Canada and ran whiskey across that same border during Prohibition. They supported wars but sold arms and goods through intermediaries to our enemies. They supported the Civil rights Movement but oppressed blacks in tenements and engaged in red-lining in the 1960's. They were a giant octopus with tentacles in everything good and bad as long as it was also profitable.

When Thom's wife, Sandra and her brother, Evan were born a year apart, the pictures all focused on their anointing as the heirs to the vast fortune.

Thom could not imagine the life they had, even with their cruel and abusive parents, they still had the best of everything. One magazine had called them the prince and princess of the Midwest.

Sandra was a gifted student and attended Harvard Medical School. Evan went to Harvard as well and graduated with a business degree.

When Sandra brought Thom home to meet the family, he remembered the suspicious looks he'd gotten. He was handsome sure but he had lost his business and was now one of their many employees.

Sandra was no winner in the looks department and the prospect of pretty grandchildren seemed to please her relatives, which did not include her parents, who were dead by then.

Evan was chilly to Thom. He was a snob and a little jealous. He was part of a famous brother/sister couple. They did everything together and suddenly, she was being photographed with Thom all over town and landing in the newspapers.

After he and Sandra got married, Evan had gotten married just a year later to a former Miss Michigan, a stunning girl from a working class family in Warren. It was then Thom knew he'd stepped into some kind of family quagmire. Who competes with his sister like that?

Evan had been a pain in the ass since then, always reminding Thom that he was an outsider and even thwarting his plan to get them on a reality show about wealthy families. The family was very conservative financially and that cash would have been all his and not more of their largess.

Thom had almost been happy when Evan died earlier this year. It was a terrible accident and he had not died right away. He lingered in the hospital for weeks before it was over.

Sandra had been so distraught, that she was hospitalized too and put in a room on the same floor as her brother.

Thom entered the dining room to find Sandra sitting alone, eating and looking upset. He still told himself that she was not a homely woman but it was no use. She had gotten none of her mother's beauty and instead took after her father, who was himself not very handsome. Her brother had gotten the looks then took them to his grave.

Thom sat across from her at the end of a long table as a staffer brought him the first course.

"Something wrong?" he asked as he began to eat.

"It's Wednesday," said Sandra with little emotion. "You're usually late on Wednesday."

"No meeting tonight," said Thom matter of factly.

"And no shower," said Sandra. "You always come home late smelling like you took a shower, but not now. Now, you just smell like… you."

"You going to start that again?" asked Thom, dropping his hand on the table hard. The handle of his knife banged loudly on the table.

"No. I don't need to, do I?" she said.

"Honey, I know you're still sad about your brother's death, but that's no reason to punish me."

"Don't say his name," said Sandra sharply. "You don't get to talk about Evan, not to me. Let me mourn in my own way."

"We're all in mourning, remember?" said Thom. "Or did you forget that? You know, I think I'll take my dinner in the study tonight."

"I'm leaving," said Sandra. "I have yoga class. You can have the room to yourself. And don't wait up for me. I may do a shift at Mercy. They're short-handed."

He started to ask her to stay, to talk and get by this but it was no use. He was wedded to her and this life and it came with both good and bad.

Thom listened to Sandra leave as the second course came. He dug into it, suddenly hungry.

9

WYANDOTTE

I finished the last of Regina's chicken as I watched DeAngela talk to a room with eight police officers in it. I was in a little office, watching a live feed on camera. I was there alone, as we did not want anyone to know I was on the case. DeAngela's team was assembled in the observation room down the hall.

These were the men and women who were deemed to have been responsible for security and surveillance the night of Ivory's death: Watch Commander Clarence Dolan and Officers, Bill Wiznewski, Lance Olof, Erica Claiborne, Rick Newson, Chance Whitehall, Jacob Vilatinni, Jamilla Cole and Dobbs Harson.

There were others there that night but these eight had direct access to cameras and equipment and should have known if a prisoner were brought in. And the officers on patrol were the only ones to come in during the gap in the surveillance.

The POA reps lined the walls and the whole thing was being recorded. Funny looking at a room full of cops, knowing one of them is a killer.

DeAngela and her team had already interviewed them separately along with every man and woman in the precinct that night. So far, they had nothing. Some conflicts existed but the blue waters were deep and so far, there was no direct evidence.

Fiona's report was still ongoing, so no one knew about the fetus except me and DeAngela and that was our ace in the whole. But in case the science did not bear us out, we had to see if we could get a break the normal way.

"So, the story we have, is the deceased just materialized in a cell between ten and six am that morning and strangled herself," said DeAngela. "No one saw her come in, no one saw her assaulted, no one filed an arrest report and she's not on any surveillance camera, which by the way, conveniently malfunctioned and has gaps in it."

DeAngela paced back and forth, looking sexy as hell in her business suit. Some of the cops were having trouble concentrating and I saw one of them checking out her ass. Couldn't blame him.

"How much longer are we gonna do this shit?" asked a POA lawyer named Harry Hunnington. He was an old hand and a damned good lawyer. "The surveillance equipment is old and the city is too damned broke to buy anything new. There was a bankruptcy in case you didn't hear."

"They told you what they know," said a female POA rep named Reid. "Make your case or don't. The clock is ticking, Ms. Gomez."

"We will," said DeAngela. "In the meantime, I'll be petitioning to switch from administrative leave with pay, to unpaid leave pending this investigation."

The room exploded in shouts and cursing. Hunnington, who was obviously the leader, calmed them all down.

"You can request anything you like, DeAngela" said Hunnington. "But if you want to stop the livelihood of any officer in this room, you will have to file for an indictment or I assure you, it won't stick."

This drew a chorus of approval from the cops and curiously, a smile from DeAngela.

She nodded to the camera and in a few seconds, the door to the room opened and in walked Jesse King, the county prosecutor's lead trial lawyer.

I smiled as I saw the faces of all the suspect cops go pale and Hunnington got out of his seat.

"What is this shit, Jesse?" asked Hunnington. "You can't be here."

"How are you Harry?" asked Jesse.

The only lawyer who might be smarter than my best buddy Marshal Jackson, is Jesse King. He's the real deal. Born just a few blocks from me and hardened in the 'hood in a way I really understood. He was incorruptible and had put away Gregory Cane, maybe the most evil man to ever walk the streets of Detroit. Cane would have guys like Every Wadson for breakfast.

"The Prosecutor, the FBI and the County Sheriff are all watching this case," said Jesse. "The whole country is watching. We have no intention for this to go cold. What happened in this precinct threatens every man in uniform in this city and perhaps the nation. I am begging you, if you know anything, please tell us now because if you do not, we will get to the bottom of this and I assure you if in the process, I find that any one of you knew something and did not divulge it, I will make sure that you go to prison without any safeguards."

The room exploded again as Jesse had just pretty much threatened to kill all of them. A cop who goes to certain prisons is a marked man for sure.

"Our clients are leaving," said Hunnington. The other lawyers all echoed this sentiment. "We did this as a courtesy. From now on, you can deal with each officer separately through their counsel."

"This is an official police interview," said Jesse. "Any man who walks out of this office could be arrested for obstruction."

"And then I will have my suspension without pay," said DeAngela.

All of the officers looked to Dolan, their Watch Commander who nodded. The ones standing sat down.

"Now," Jesse continued. "If any officer wants to contact me, you can, and I assure you none of your brothers will know who it was. For now, the IAD has another hour for you to be here. Take some time and think about it."

Jesse walked out and DeAngela left with him, leaving the cops stunned.

I had been watching very carefully and my head was filled with stuff. I had the files on all of them and I knew a couple of them personally. I wish I could say I knew which one of them did it, but this was not like a box of chicken. Whoever murdered Ivory was smart, cold and had help. It had to be more than one of them but which ones?

Dolan was probably only there because he was responsible for the precinct. You could see on his face that he knew he had just drawn the duty that night. He'd been a real badass when he was on the street and had dodged a big corruption scandal some years ago. He had two ex-wives and was working on a third.

Bill Wiznewski was a vet and a solid family man with a bunch of kids. He had a good rep but was a bit of a religious fanatic. I saw him sometimes dropping off my father at Mass. He was working back up to Dolan and had dodged that same corruption scandal.

Erica Claiborne was a relative newbie and was already in law school, angling for a prosecutor's job down the road. She was tough and determined but had no taste for street duty which was odd because she was one of the best shots on the force and had won two contests. She'd been on administrative that night.

Lance Olof had been a street cop but was known to be violent and exhibited bad judgment. He was taken off active when he discharged his weapon and almost killed a kid holding a Red Bull. He was in the twenty percent that I would get rid of.

Olof worked surveillance under Rick Newson, who could not explain the malfunction. Newson was generally a good guy but had some bad habits, like he was a gambler and had gotten caught with a low rent hooker once, which meant he did it all the time.

Whitehall I knew from around the force. We had worked together on tac squads and I always found him to be capable and even headed which was no surprise because he had been in Special Ops in Afghanistan.

Vilatinni was a bad egg and we all knew it. He was one of those guys you expected to be found shot or worse. IAD had been trying to get rid of him for years but Vilatinni was too smart and people loved the guy. I knew he was bent but I liked him, too.

Jamilla Cole was a good cop who was well thought of but had a problem with authority figures. She'd been reprimanded a few times and was known to have a rather short fuse.

Dobbs Harson was a lot like Vilatinni. Although no one had ever accused him of being bent, he did bend the rules and was known to be a ladies man, which put him high on my list.

Whitehall, Vilatinni, Cole and Harson had all come in during the window when we think Ivory was sneaked in. These four were seen leaving, but no camera ever caught them coming in the precinct.

All of them seemed guilty to me and I had a random thought of just beating it out of them one by one. Then I saw something that got my attention.

Two sets of the cops were partners: Whitehall and Vilatinni and Cole and Harson. One team sat close together and talked with the same lawyer who represented both of them but the other team was totally different.

Jamilla Cole and Dobbs Harson were on opposite sides of the room and each had gotten their own lawyer.

Dobbs Harson talked frantically to his lawyer but Jamilla sat stone-faced. They had sat next to each other when DeAngela and Jesse addressed them but as soon as they left, they had separated without a word.

A police partnership was a sacred thing, almost like family. Sometimes partners were not close or drifted apart but usually that would end the relationship.

Cole and Harson were riding together and as far as I knew, there was no trouble in paradise— until now.

There was a soft knock on the door and then Jesse King and DeAngela walked in.

"Hope you don't mind but I told Jesse," said DeAngela.

"No," I said. Jesse and I shook hands.

"I'm not for you being involved, Danny," said Jesse.

"I could guess that," I said. "But you don't have to worry about me killing the suspect."

"See, but I do worry, Danny," said Jesse. "If I were in your shoes, I don't know what I'd do."

"I'm afraid you're stuck with me," I said. "Unless you plan to renege on our deal, DeAngela."

"Nope," she said looking a Jesse.

"Out voted, counselor," I said.

"Okay," said Jesse. "We got the fetus but if we get into this and jeopardy attaches, we're fucked if the science doesn't hold up."

"Which is why we need a break," said DeAngela. "Don't try the case before its time, Jesse."

"I don't think our scare tactic worked," said Jesse. "So, do you have anything, Danny?"

And I'll be damned if Jesse was not right about me because my first thought was not to tell them what I had just seen. I'd follow Cole and Harson and then force them into talking. Or maybe me and Vinny and one of her brothers would pay them a visit. It felt real good but it would not be playing with the team.

"Let everyone go except Jamilla Cole," I said.

"Why?" asked DeAngela.

"I think she and her partner are dirty," I said, "but I think she's covering for him and she's pissed about it."

"Shit," said Jesse checking out the camera feed. "They're not even looking at each other. Good catch, detective."

"Then we question her?" asked DeAngela.

"No," said Jesse. "We don't say anything, I mean nothing. Then we release her. Her partner won't believe we just sat there and said nothing and distrust will settle in."

"If he did it, he might move on Jamilla or whoever he's working with," I said.

"Goddamn cops are scary people," said DeAngela. "Okay, let's do it."

They left and soon, I saw them enter the room with the cops. DeAngela let them all go but asked Jamilla to stay behind. Jamilla, her lawyer and Dobbs Harson and his lawyer all protested but in the end, Jamilla was left in the room alone with her attorney, the IAD officer and the county's top prosecutor.

Jesse and DeAngela said nothing for five minutes. Jamilla's lawyer kept asking them questions but they said nothing. When they released her, Dobbs Harson was waiting in the hallway. I could hear them arguing as they left.

Jesse was clever. Even if Jamilla's lawyer said that Jesse and DeAngela just sat there, no one would believe him. It was his job to win and lying about it would be protecting his client. Jesse had just used their own attorney/client privilege against them.

Now, the IAD would sit on Jamilla and Dobbs and wait for something to happen. Not a bad strategy but it might not bear any fruit.

My cell phone rang. It was Erik and so I didn't dare ignore it.

"Sup boss?" I said.

"Got a new case, a homicide and I want you on it," said Erik. "I'm sending details to your cell."

"Cool but—"

"Just go, Danny. We'll talk later."

****

I left the IAD offices making sure not to be spotted by anyone. I ended up walking out of the service area into a stinking alley. This is what it's like when you work against your brothers, I thought.

I walked back to my car and pulled off, headed to I-75. The case I was put on had actually taken place in another city.

Wyandotte is south of Detroit, bordering the river, what we call downriver. Don't know much about it, only that it's the second oldest city in the state, something they brag about as if anyone gives a shit.

Someone had dumped a body near the old Oak Street Union Station landmark. The Wyandotte Police don't get many murders in a city of only twenty-five thousand.

I pulled up to the crime scene which had already been roped off. I got out of my car and walked past the onlookers, who braved the cold just to have something to tweet and text about.

The body had been left in some thick weeds and was discovered by a city maintenance crew.

I was summoned by a uniformed officer and I noticed that there was no detective on scene. Shit, did they even have one in Wyandotte?

"Officer Steve Baker, detective," said a fresh-faced kid who looked right out of the academy.

"Cavanaugh," I said.

"I know, sir," said Baker. "I read about you last year. Some doings, huh? That's my partner, Nelson. He's been keeping the people at bay. Damned cell phone cameras."

We walked over to the body which was being readied for transport.

"My boss talked to yours and we're taking this," I said.

"That's what they're telling me," said Baker. "Don't know why."

The deceased was a black male and had been worked over pretty good. He'd been beaten with something and three of his fingers were mangled, probably broken. His face was bruised and swollen and he had been bound hand and foot.

"Do we know who he is?"

"Yes sir," said Baker. "Raymond Ranier."

"RaRa," I said to myself. "Yes, this is one of ours."

"The chief wants to go co on it," said Baker. "I'm the primary here."

I drew in a deep breath and let it out as I stooped to get a better look. So, this is where Ivory's missing friend had gone.

"I'm betting you didn't find his cell phone," I said.

"Nope," said Baker. "Kid's got I.D., wallet even had money in it. So, I'm guessing this was not a robbery."

"No, it wasn't," I said.

I wanted to tell him who this corpse was and why DPD was interested but there was no need to give the media more ways to sensationalize this.

"This kid's a missing person," I said. "Probably killed by some bad folks in the D and dumped here hoping you guys wouldn't call us."

"Shit," said Baker. "Premeditated?"

"I'll get our people out here for the body and I'll take the wallet and ID," I said.

I called DeAngela and told her the news.

"I knew it," she said. "I was in denial but I knew that kid was dead."

"How long before the press knows?" I asked.

"I can get them to hold off for a few days but not much longer."

"I'll send Fiona and her team to his apartment to see what they find. Then, I'll follow up."

I called Fiona and told her team to go to RaRa's apartment and give it the treatment before I got there. I told her to make sure there was no one there when I came in later.

I waited for the morgue guys, then drove back to Detroit behind them. On the way, I started to call Vinny to tell her the bad news. Then for some reason, I didn't want to talk on my cell. All cops are paranoid and when it kicks in, we don't ignore it.

I veered off the freeway and drove back home and picked Vinny up.

RMC was in good hands as the family was still swarming our place since Ivory's death. Marcus Sr. was planning a funeral and I was dreading it. I hate funerals and none are worse than black or Irish ones.

We got into my car. Vinny had her gun and badge. She was a reserve cop and so could still carry by law.

It was kinda nice being her partner again. But I was worried. Since the baby, I had lost some of my edge. It was okay when it was just me but what if something happened to us both?

"I've been waiting for news all day," said Vinny. "I wanted to call but I know it's not cool."

"We got eight suspects and we found that missing friend of Ivory's, dead, tortured, I think."

"RaRa's dead? Jesus. I liked him."

"I'm gonna lose RaRa's case to IAD, but we have a minute to get as much as we can. They didn't find his phone and I think he gave it up to them during the torture. They only broke three fingers on one hand."

"Damn," said Vinny. "Some serious players here. Ivory's phone was gone too, but we know from her records she and RaRa talked before she was killed."

"So what was the killer looking for?" I asked almost to myself. "More than likely, evidence of who they are."

"A voicemail or something?" asked Vinny.

"That's what I'm thinking," I said. "RaRa was an IT kid so he might have made a copy."

Later, we got Fiona's text saying the place was done. We took a trip downtown and visited RaRa's place.

It was a very nice loft over what used to be a bank. RaRa was a coder for Compuware, apparently, it paid well.

We broke the yellow crime scene tape as we entered. His place had been trashed of course, because the killers had already been there. I figured that but I wasn't looking for the same thing as they were.

If RaRa had evidence, he would not leave it in his home, at least, I hoped he wasn't that dumb.

Vinny was wearing some jeans and a black t-shirt under her coat and her hair was tied back. I was trying not to notice how good she looked and how seeing her in action with that gun on her hip was making me feel some kinda way.

Suddenly, I felt her hand on my arm as I was checking a pile of debris.

"I'm loving being back in action," said Vinny smiling a little. "Just like old times."

"Don't start nothing you can't finish up in here," I said smiling back.

That got me a hard slap on the ass as she walked away.

After an hour, we gave up. Vinny and I had guessed that if a guy like RaRa had evidence, he would've felt safer hiding it somewhere in the digital space.

"His computer is trashed," I said. "Maybe the killer thought the same thing."

"Of course he did," said Vinny. "He's a cop. Let's check out Compuware."

RaRa's workplace was not far from where he lived. We were let inside by his supervisor, a man named Madrillian.

They had not only gotten his phone, they got RaRa to give up his password and had remotely erased all of his files at work, including valuable projects RaRa had been working on.

We did not find any additional email addresses or accounts and all of his social media had been shut down. Someone had erased RaRa from the face of the digital planet.

RaRa's supervisor was shocked and could barely speak as we peppered him with questions.

As we were leaving, I stopped suddenly and sighed.

"What?" asked Vinny.

"I'm losing it," I said. "Family. There's nothing at his place, work or in his wallet about family, no pictures or anything."

"Maybe he doesn't have any," said Vinny. "Then again, even a ward of the state has foster family."

We went back and asked for RaRa's employee file. Ivory was surprisingly listed as his emergency contact along with several other friends. And there was a reference to his mother, Delores Ranier but she had no address.

"Prison?" asked Vinny.

"Or drug addict," I said.

We checked the prison system and found Delores but she had been let out a year ago. Then we checked the halfway house she'd been released to. She had registered and then been moved by her son to a place called Second Chances not far from RaRa's loft.

Suddenly, I felt sorry for RaRa. He'd come from a bad situation was blessed with brains but that had not saved him. And I hated to say it but he loved Ivory, who was in her own way, just as no good as his mother.

We went to Second Chances but Delores had been gone for over a month. She'd fallen off the wagon and broken parole. We checked her old room but found nothing.

We walked out of Second Chances as the sun was setting. We were both tired but we had no choice but to keep going. Once news got out that the killer had taken out another innocent black kid, Detroit was going to be knee-deep in trouble.

"You know this area?" Vinny asked.

"Some," I said. "But the dope houses change a lot. We could be out here all night."

"Then, we'd better get going if we want to find her," said Vinny.

Without even thinking, we both checked our weapons. I pulled the .45 and the Glock and realized that I had not fired either in a long time and if I did, it would be the first time since my son was born.

As we got ready to go into the night, Vinny looked over to me and I saw that same awareness in her eyes.

She kissed me and though it was strange, I was very happy to return it. And although I knew she meant it as a bond of solidarity, I could not help but think that it was a kiss goodbye.

PART TWO:

DEATH CITY

"I don't know. It think it's
one of them gray areas."

- Kelvin

10

PAYMENT

He listened as the shower went on in the little motel room he'd rented for the evening's activities. He could no longer risk doing things like this in his church and even though he had a second home, he couldn't do it there either. His wife probably had the place staked out.

Why that woman cared so much about his business was a mystery. Women. As soon as they got old, all they cared about was where your dick was going. He had not dumped her ass. Why couldn't she be happy with that?

The Reverend Samuel D. Paymer was not the kind of man to live without the things he needed and this little tryst was one of them.

God was mysterious and he was also cruel. All the things people liked were forbidden. Thank goodness for redemption, he thought. And he was going to have to do some serious praying for what he was about to do tonight.

It had been a month since he'd seen Impala and he was going to make up for all the lost time. He'd taken a pill an hour ago and so he was as stiff as a board and ready.

Paymer thought about the first time he saw her, running for the bus in her little short skirt, hair flying behind her. She looked like a school girl.

Impala missed her bus and it took him fifteen minutes to persuade her to ride with him. Three hours later, he had that little skirt hiked up and her bent over his desk in the back of his church office.

He'd had girlfriends before, mostly from the church but they were always dangerous with their big ass mouths and self-righteousness. Impala was a pro and so he paid her to keep her ass off the street and service him.

He knew she cheated, but she was careful about it and so he didn't quibble. Beggars could definitely not be choosers in his delicate situation.

Paymer was sixty and not in very good shape. He was overweight and had the Black Trinity: hypertension, diabetes and high cholesterol. He took all kinds of pills and so now needed help in the erection department, which he didn't mind at all. God provided by science and so it was just a matter of which pill you favored.

He'd been a basketball player back in the day, but was never tall enough or good enough to make it big. He'd served in the Army but nothing came of it, except he became a Chaplin, which led him to a deaconship at his local church after the Gulf War.

After a few years of service, he'd gotten a little storefront church and it wasn't long before he was pastoring at a bigger place.

Mount Holy Grace was a pretty tired name for a church but all the good names were taken. He didn't want a name with *blood* in it or some kind of biblical term. Try getting old black people to write ecumenical or ecclesiastical on a check.

Running a church was a lot like running a drug crew, he thought. He was selling a needed product, creating a dependency and then servicing it for a price. It was very cynical to think this way, but it was hard out there for a pastor these days. Between the Mega churches and Oprah Sunday, everyone was cutting into his profits more and more.

The only thing he didn't like about religion were all the arcane restrictions. All the pastors he knew had sidechicks, drank or smoked dope. It was a shame that they had to hide their humanity but that was part of the deal. People wanted to believe that they could be better, like their leaders.

The other reason he was sneaking around motels was that fuckin' gangster, Renardo. Paymer had peeped Renardo's real estate game and would be damned if that lowlife thug would steal from his people. He had put the word out not to deal with Renardo and to turn their dollars back to the church instead.

Paymer has instructed Sister Temple to rescind their deal and that bastard had threatened to kill her, or at least that's what Sister Temple had said.

Changes were coming to the city and he would be damned if the criminals would take a foothold in his city again.

"What you doin' in there woman?" yelled Paymer as he felt the rigidness of his erection become slightly uncomfortable. He needed to get this thing off quick so they could rest and get another one in before he had to go back home.

He dreaded that. His wife was not feeling him lately and every time he came home late, he got shit from her. He planned to just go to the guest room and not even bother with her later.

The shower turned off and he heard the shower door creak open slowly.

"'Bout goddamned time," he mumbled.

Impala walked out a moment later, still wet and wearing a towel. She was early twenties, brown-skinned and very pretty even without makeup.

"Dry off and get over here, woman," Paymer ordered. "I ain't got a lot of time."

Impala said nothing and in fact, had a look of fright on her face as she stepped aside in a strange motion. From behind her, Renardo walked out and behind him was Kelvin, holding a sawed-off shotgun.

"What in the—?" said Paymer.

"They came in the window," said Impala, her voice shaking.

"I cut my damned hand taking that grate off the window," said Kelvin. "I should shoot your ass for that." Kelvin had a hotel hand towel wrapped around one hand with a bright red stain on it.

"Get in that bed with your man," said Renardo.

Impala walked over to the bed and gingerly climbed in next to Paymer who had a look of abject anger on his face.

Renardo whipped out a cell phone and took a picture of them.

"I must look awful," said Impala.

"Shut up!" snapped Paymer.

"Watch ya mouth," said Renardo. "It's not her fault."

"You look good," said Kelvin.

"What the fuck do you want?" said Paymer.

Renardo was silent for a second. He took a deep breath, calming himself.

"Impala, what do you see in this lying ass thief of a minister?" asked Renardo.

Impala looked to Reverend Paymer with innocence and a little fear.

"Don't look at him," said Renardo. *"I* asked you a question."

"He's good to me," said Impala. "A girl needs some kindness in this city."

"Especially when she has a dick," said Renardo flatly.

Impala winced a little as if mildly insulted and then: "Yes, especially when she's got one."

"Man," said Kelvin, "if you didn't have a johnson, I would swear you was a woman."

"I am a woman," said Impala quickly. "I'm just not complete, not yet."

"And I bet this piece of shit next to you has been promising to take care of that for you," said Renardo.

"Well, he's lying. He doesn't want you to change. He wants that dick."

"Get on with it," said Paymer impatiently.

"You ain't in no position to be giving orders, Payment," said Renardo. "Mind yourself or it will get ugly up in here. Now, what I want is for you to stay out of my business or that picture of you and Impala here will be posted on your church's Facebook Page and Twitter account, only we will block out Impala's face because I can see that he/she is a nice person."

"Too good for you, Reverend Payment," said Kelvin resting the shotgun across one forearm but still pointed at Paymer.

"You can prey on the people of this city but men like you always get caught," said Paymer. "God will—"

"I will have Kelvin shoot you if you dare to tell me what God's gonna do," said Renardo. "You laying here in a bed with a big ass hard on, next to a naked man. I think it's safe to say that God ain't listening to your faggot ass right now."

"Sam Jackson cold!" said Kelvin laughing.

"You caught me at a bad time, Payment," Renardo continued. "Everybody in my business is acting like a goddamned fool these days and they are forcing me to go back to my old ways. You are going to give me what I've lost on the deals you scared off. I will settle your debt for ten thousand, cash and I want it a week from now."

Paymer mumbled something under his breath.

"Excuse me?" said Renardo. "Didn't catch that."

"Fine," said Paymer.

"Also, Impala here is coming with us tonight," said Renardo. "You give him the money 'cause I know he ain't doing your old ass for free. You go home to your family and think about what you've done."

Paymer was fuming but he reached for his pants and gave Impala a wad of cash, which she held tentatively while looking at Paymer like a child.

"Go on," said Paymer. "Go."

"Get dressed," said Renardo. "And Rev, if we check on Impala here and see one mark on his pretty face, we're coming for you."

"He's not like that," said Impala a little angry. "He don't hit me. I'm not that thirsty."

"My bad," said Renardo. "My bad."

Impala got dressed in the bathroom and walked a few minutes later. Kelvin was right. Dressed up, you could not tell she was complicated.

"Have a good night, Rev," said Renardo as he and Kelvin left the motel room with Impala.

They walked out into the parking lot, then to the rear where they had parked.

"I bet old boy is in there jacking off," said Kelvin laughing.

Impala shivered as the air hit her. She was wearing a skirt and a waist length faux fur.

"Cold as shit out here," she said. "Damn."

Impala sat up front with Kelvin, while Renardo rode in the rear. Kelvin turned on the car and pumped up the heat.

"Take me to the Denny's over on Eight Mile," said Impala almost like an order. "And thanks for fucking up my night, niggas. Now he's gonna want double the next time."

"I knew that little girl thing was an act," said Renardo. "No way a working girl like you is that soft."

"All part of the package," said Impala heartily. "I'm selling more than ass. A man likes to think he's in charge, makes him like it more."

"What you packin' for defense?" asked Kelvin.

"Fuck with me and find out," said Impala.

This made Renardo and Kelvin both roar with laughter.

"So, when y'all do it, does the Rev do you or do you do him?" asked Renardo. "I got to know."

"No kiss and tell," said Impala. "We get it in and get it done. Thanks for making him pay me. I need to get a resupply and my connection got busted. Where can a girl score some shit?"

"What kind?" asked Kelvin.

"I need weed, Oxy, Vikes," said Impala.

"Damn, you starting a pharmacy?" said Renardo.

"My clients like it and I sell a little on the side. I like shoes," she said.

"Well, there's Money Mike over by Nevada and Six," said Kelvin. "That girl Jarindah's crew rolls by Mound and thereabouts. But I don't like that bitch. And my man Jimmy, the Samoan."

"Watch out for him" said Renardo. "He likes to cheat people, dirty motherfucker. Almost had to shoot his big ass once."

"You know, you finer than my last three bitches," said Kelvin. "When you get completed you need to check a brother out."

Impala could not help but to laugh at this. Her voice was soft and light like a woman but there was a huskier undertone to it.

"I'll schedule you," said Impala. She flipped down the blinder and looked at herself in the mirror.

"Sorry," said Renardo, "but if you get with him, you'd be doing a man. He was born one way and can't nothing on this Earth change that."

"But if he ain't got no dick and there's a hole, then it's all good," said Kelvin.

"No, that would make you a homo," said Renardo. "Plain and simple."

"I don't know. I think it's one of them gray areas," said Kelvin.

"No, it ain't!" said Renardo a little upset. "What the fuck is wrong with you?"

"Impala, what you think?" asked Kelvin.

"The heart wants what it wants," said Impala. "And so does the dick."

"You know, there was a time, I woulda just kicked your ass for not being normal," said Renardo. "You know, on general principle, but I'm on this thing of trying to be a better person, more enlightened and shit. You can't help what you are. It's like being born with one of them fucked up baby arms or retarded. So, I'm respectin' the universe and not going there."

"Hurrah for you," said Impala crossing her legs and she caught Kelvin peeking at them.

"See, that was sarcastic," said Renardo, "but I'm not letting it get to me. People been trying my nerves lately but I'm gonna stay in control."

"He really is a changed man," said Kelvin. "You just don't know. Last year, well, I can't really say, but let's just say last year was cray cray."

"So, you ain't got nothing to say about what just went down back there with the Rev?" asked Renardo.

"None of my business," said Impala. "I know the kind of man he is. He don't judge me and I don't judge him. Whatever this is between the two of you, I'm sure he brought it on himself. The Reverend is full of fake pride about stuff. I just do me and move on."

"That's a good way to be," said Renardo. "Wouldn't want to have to come looking for you."

"There is it right there," said Impala.

Kelvin pulled into the Denny's, which was very crowded. Impala fixed her face in the mirror again.

"Thank you for a lovely evening," she said. And then she got out and walked inside.

Renardo got into the front seat and watched her walk in.

"She's gonna go right back to him," said Kelvin. "You know that."

"That's her problem," said Renardo. "He's out of my business and I now I gotta decide what to do about Thom."

"I say we take the money, then fuck him up," said Kelvin. "We can't let that shit stand."

"How does that get me my dream?" asked Renardo. "How does that set me up for life, which is what I was promised?"

"It don't but you'll feel better," said Kelvin.

"Thom ain't gonna make it that easy," said Renardo. "He ain't no punk. He knows people now and he's from a rich family…"

"What?" asked Kelvin when Renardo didn't continue.

"Thom ain't the one we should be concentrating on. I pretended to negotiate with him to put him at ease while I thought about what I was gonna do but I got it. We take the wife."

"We kill her?" asked Kelvin.

"Get the wax out of your ears, dumbass. I said we *take* her. We kidnap the bitch."

"Oh, snap," said Kelvin. "This is like why we had all that research on him."

"Yes," said Renardo a little exasperated. "Just in case something like this happened. This is part of my new thing. The old me would just wing it, but it's good to be prepared."

Renardo pulled out his cell phone and pulled up a file. In it was a breakdown of everything they knew about Thom Ross.

Thom had a mistress who lived in Ann Arbor and she had a little girl. He went by to hit it twice a month usually on a Wednesday. He liked to gamble but only in Canada for some reason. He had drinking and golfing buddies and generally led a privileged white man's life.

His wife, was a doctor whose family was old money rich. She was homely and fancied herself some kind of do-gooder. She had a brother she shared the family money with. Parents were dead.

"Remember when we followed her. She got that yoga class," said Renardo. "We can get her there."

"But she don't have no regular night," said Kelvin.

"Then we go every night until we see the bitch," said Renardo. "Get the place ready. I'm about to show Thom that you do not go back on your word to me. Okay, let's roll."

They drove away. A moment after they pulled off, Impala left the restaurant and pulled up her Über app so she could go back to the reverend.

11

SLAP

To find a drug addict, you have to think like one. A dopefiend is like a really smart child. They are clever, but their logic is always juvenile and they tend to leave obvious clues because they are ashamed of themselves.

We could have been looking for RaRa's mother, Delores, forever if we didn't know this. We knew that she would be using somewhere close to her son's apartment in case she got into trouble or needed to steal something from him or compromise him in some way. An addict's loved ones are always the best source for exploitation.

Delores didn't have a car and was on foot, so notwithstanding a car service, she probably took the bus looking to score. We followed the bus route to the first bad stretch of neighborhood and started asking around.

Contrary to what people believe, there is no rule against snitching in the 'hood. A man or woman will drop on you in a second for money. It's only when people are watching that you will find tight lips.

We got three houses quickly. The first one had two armed guards and juvie lookouts. This was a sell house and the users could stay for a fee. No way Delores was in there, we thought. Too expensive.

The second one looked better. It was actually an abandoned row of commercial buildings that were marked for renovation. In the meantime, the Bergman Building was a communal flop house and whatever else locals could think of. The power was rigged and the heat probably was, too.

"Big place," I said. "We could be here a while."

"If they don't all run," said Vinny.

"I say we tell the truth. A man's dead and we're looking for a next of kin."

"You're getting soft, Cavanaugh," she smiled. "Time was, you'd just plow through until you got what you wanted."

"Just trying to keep it simple," I said. "And I ain't the one killed a dude in our backyard."

"Not gonna let me forget that, are you?" Vinny said.

"Not for a while," I responded.

Someone had put a hit on me in a case and made the mistake of trying to do it at my home. We caught him in the backyard and Vinny, barefoot and pregnant, had put one in his head.

We got out of the car around the corner from the place. We parked under a streetlight and made sure to leave my DPD sign in the window. We walked the block to the buildings.

"Smell that?" asked Vinny. "Barbecue."

Someone was grilling nearby and the smell was wafting all over, carried by the wind. Whatever it was, it was pungent and gamey.

The front of the place was guarded by an unarmed kid about sixteen or so. He was overweight and mixed race and had that look of desolation about him. It's in the eyes, a belief that there is nothing good to come. Tilt that one way, and the guy's a lost soul. Go the other way, and he's a killer.

This kid was the first kind, not dangerous but he'd accepted that his life was never gonna matter.

"Nickel entry," said the kid. "Pop que-ing back there."

I handed the kid a five. He pocketed it and pointed to a narrow passage between buildings that led to the back of the place.

"We lookin' for a lady," I said. "Her boy is hurt bad and she don't know about it."

"Delores," said Vinny.

"I don't be gettin' names," said the kid, "but it's several females called "D" one way or another."

Me and Vinny headed down the narrow walkway and as we did, the food smell became stronger and we could hear talking, cheering and music.

At the end of the walkway, a man stepped out. He had the same look as the kid out front, but tilted the bad way. Vinny tensed behind me. She felt it too.

"What y'all wont?" asked the man. He had a hard, craggy face. He'd seen some shit, I thought.

"Looking for somebody," I said.

"We don't do that and if ya'll cops, you need a warrant. We squatters back here."

"A woman's son is dead and she doesn't know," said Vinny. "We're just here to tell her."

"Look, y'all know folks doin' stuff back here. We don't need no trouble."

Normally, this is where I'd show him my badge or better the gun and shit would go left, but we were not trying to have a damned shootout over finding a junkie.

"Let me give you a name and you tell me if we can see her," I said. "Delores Ranier."

The big man's face showed recognition but there was something not right about it. Vinny tensed again and I felt it too.

"D-Lo be with my man Jimmy," said the man. "You gon' 'hafta talk to him 'bout all that. He run the fight corner over there. Can't miss him, he the biggest thing out here."

The guard stepped aside and we walked in to what used to be the parking lot of the place. It was like a little marketplace and village.

Drug use was everywhere and right in the middle, was an old white man barbecuing his ass off. He had a huge oil drum grill and a long line of people waiting to buy a plate.

"I think that's goat he's cooking," said Vinny. "Daddy used to cook those in a pit back in the day."

"I've dug a pit or two," I said. "Been a while since I had that."

"That's got to be him," said Vinny pointing to a big crowd in the northeast corner where the cheering was coming from.

There was a circle drawn with paint and in it, two men fought bare-handed, while the crowd bet and cheered the men on. You could see dried blood in the circle, history of the fights before.

PART ONE: LIFE CITY

A Samoan with an afro sat on a raised bench watching the spectacle. He was big like a lot of Samoan men and he had that hard bent look about him as well.

I knew there were a few local bare knuckle fight clubs in the city but I didn't know who was running the east side one, until now.

We walked over and were met by two men who patted us down. We told them we were armed and one of them ran over to Jimmy who walked over with three more men.

"Y'all need to raise up," said Jimmy. "We don't want no trouble and this is private property."

"We need to see D-Lo," I said.

One of them produced a gun and held it down by his side.

"We're asking," said Vinny. "It's about her son. He's dead."

"Y'all off duty?" asked Jimmy.

"Yeah," I said. "Not trying to violate people for living."

Some of the men laughed and this eased the tension a little. Jimmy was thinking now and he could see we weren't here for trouble.

I had already calculated how I would shoot them if it got crazy. I'd move to my right, away from the one with the gun, while pulling the Glock with my left hand. Vinny would draw her weapon to my right. She'd hit the armed man and I would put one in Jimmy's fat ass head. By then, the .45 would be out too and I'd catch one of the other men with it. Vinny would shoot another and then I'd just fire until no one was left standing.

"D-Lo belongs to me for the rest of this month," said Jimmy. "She owes me and she's working it off."

We both knew what this meant. Delores was turning tricks for Jimmy on a drug debt. We also knew that she'd never be able to fully pay it off and would just ease into indentured servitude to the Samoan until she was no good to him.

Vinny was pissed about this. She had a thing about women's issues and she saw a lot of this shit in the city, where women were treated like some kind of second-rate currency.

I gave her a look to say that she should let me talk. She would start cursing and then we'd never get out of here without violence.

"We'll pay it," I said. "She's got to do the next of kin thing and we need to close this out."

"How did he die?" asked Jimmy. "I thought he was some kind of computer kid."

"Somebody killed him, robbery. His boss is a big shot in case you were wondering why we're here." I lied knowing the truth would be wasted on these guys.

"How about this," said Jimmy. "I let her go and you owe me a favor."

"Can't do that," I said. "I ain't got it like that and I don't lie to people no matter what they do for a living."

"A woman lost her boy," said Vinny. "Don't that mean nothing to you?"

"Bitch got a big ass mouth," said one of Jimmy's men, a guy with a mane of dreads and big arms. "Might have to put something in it."

The other men all laughed and I was hot. I know it was silly and Vinny can take care of herself but I was raised just like these men and I couldn't help it. He insulted my woman and I take that shit personally.

"Vollo, what did I tell you about talking?" said Jimmy. "Apologize to the sister."

"Fuck dat," said Vollo. "Men are talking here. This ho need to be silent."

More laughter from the men and I could see Jimmy was enjoying it too.

"I apologize for him," said Jimmy. "We don't insult women as fine as you."

"How about I go a round with Vollo here," I said suddenly. "He looks like a fighter. I win, Delores comes with us. I lose and I owe you that favor and we pay her debt."

Jimmy and the crew liked this idea as I knew they would. It was not the greatest thing I ever came up with but I was very pent up about things and I needed an outlet for my aggression and I did not like this Vollo.

If I won, then fine but even if I lost, I'd still get what we came for, I'd just have to pay for it. Jimmy didn't realize that my offer was a scam. He just liked the action.

"We do three rounds here," said Jimmy.

"I'll only need one," I said. "If he makes it out, you win."

Now there was cheering and more laughter as the betting started. Vollo was looking at me with anger as he had just been insulted. Jimmy looked at Vollo, who nodded eagerly as if to say he was sure he could beat me.

Vinny nodded to me. She was down with it and I couldn't tell if it was because we needed Delores or because she had been insulted.

"One five minute round," said Jimmy. "Vollo, you get the usual pay if you win."

"If?" said Vollo snickering. "Negro, please. This White Hope won't last a minute."

I got into the circle and took off my coat. It was cold but we'd be working up heat soon. Vinny took my weapons. I saw her flip the safety off the Glock. Smart girl.

There are two kinds of fighters. The first kind was a guy who thought he was tough when he was just mean, angry and big. He liked hurting other people and the power he got just being unafraid of confrontation.

The second kind of fighter has made peace with his inner animal and is ready to die or kill every time he squares up. He fights because he has to and he wants to win because he has conviction.

I was the second kind of fighter and if Vollo was too, then I was about to take an ass-whupping. And so I kept telling myself that no matter what, I'd get my anger out and I'd get Delores. But don't get it twisted, I wanted to whip his loud-mouthed disrespectful ass.

The match started and I waited as the crowd got into it. Street fighters are given to spectacle and so I knew he'd want to put on a show. I was taller and heavier but he was younger and probably faster. He thought this was an advantage. Maybe in a foot race, but not necessarily in a fight.

Vollo threw some measuring punches and I caught them easily. They had power and they hurt even when deflected. He grinned and danced trying to look bad.

I was thinking about Koney the bully and how fights are usually quick.

Suddenly, I shot out a hand a hit him in the face but it was not a fist. It was a slap.

Smack!

The crowd gasped because women are slapped like that. Vollo got angry and waded in catching me with a hook to my side and another blow that grazed my temple. I saw this second shot coming but I let it hit because he had twisted his body over his stance in his anger at my insult and before he could get back…

Smack!

A backhand to the other side of his face. The crowd reacted again, only this time there was laughter in the mix.

Well, Vollo was definitely the first kind of fighter because now he was hot. I wanted him to be. The brothers are easily put off their game by humiliation. They get so much of it indirectly each day, that it was a tipping point when it was direct.

"Easy Vollo!" yelled Jimmy from behind me.

Vollo bolted at me and lunged just like Koney did. It was so fast, that he almost caught me off guard.

He met my right hand on the bridge of his nose.
Vollo fell backwards on his ass. When he got up, I was
on him and this time I slammed a fist into the side of
his head. He wobbled and fell to one knee. He tried to
get up but kept falling.

I went to him and grabbed him by the dreads and
slapped the shit out of him again, then I hooked him
hard to the jaw and he went down for good.

The crowd groaned and gasped and cursed. Money
changed hands and I could see Jimmy was not happy.

I went over to Vinny and put on my guns and coat
and walked calmly over to the Samoan. My hands were
red and already bruising. I felt good.

"Who the fuck are you?" asked Jimmy.

"Just a concerned citizen tonight," I said. "Where's
Delores?"

I could see Jimmy thinking about going back on our
deal. But if he did that, his word would mean nothing
to his people and he'd lose face.

"Green van second row. Tell that bitch to stay way
from my shit," he said. "I mean it."

"I can see you're a standup guy," I said. "So, I'll give
you that favor as long as it don't involve a homicide.
Ask for me and I'll do what I can." I handed him a card.

Jimmy and me looked at each other and he could see
I was not lying. Every man in the city has a code and
it's either good or bad.

"Bet," said Jimmy glad to have gotten something out
of all this, which made his men look at him with respect
because of my respect to him. "What's your name?"

"Cavanaugh."

PART ONE: LIFE CITY

Vinny and I walked towards the vans while Jimmy's men pulled Vollo off the ground.

"You need to put some cold on those hands," said Vinny. She grabbed my arm and I knew I'd be getting me some later. Women were always turned on by shit like this.

Delores Ranier was a thin, brown-skinned woman with a short haircut over what used to be a cute face. Drug use and a hard life had stolen her beauty as it always does.

Her little feathered cut looked fresh. Black women and their hair fascinated me. Here she was, a drug addict sold into urban slavery, turning tricks and yet she had found some woman in this squatters' house to do her hair.

Delores stood smoking cigarettes with two other women by a green van which was rocking as one of her other sisters was in there working.

"Delores?" I asked.

"Who wants to know?" she said.

"I'm Detective Cavanaugh and this is Officer Shaw. We're here about your son, Raymond."

Before we told her anything, I saw recognition in her eyes. All mothers in cities like Detroit dreaded a visit from the police and those words.

Delores began to shake and just started to cry. She fell and I caught her before she hit the ground. We each took an arm and easily carried her away as she sobbed.

We went back to the front of the place and we let Delores stand on her own.

"Can you walk?" I asked.

"What's wrong with her?" asked the kid at the front.

We didn't answer. We just moved up the street, back towards our car around the corner.

"He's dead, isn't he?" asked Delores.

"Yes, ma'am," said Vinny. "We're sorry."

"I knew it," said Delores. "It's my fault. I was never no good to the boy." She sobbed again.

"Delores, we need you to hold it together," said Vinny. "I know this is bad, but I've lost my sister too, the same way. We both have to be—"

Vinny was a little surprised to see I had both guns out and I had moved in front of her.

We'd left our car under a street light. But as we got to the corner, I could see no light coming from where we had left our ride.

This is one of those things people who live in the city noticed. Someone had knocked out the light. If they saw the police sign on it, why would they do that unless…

Vinny whipped out her gun and pushed Delores back as we got to the corner. I tossed Vinny my keys and nodded to her. She knew what I was going to do.

"What's going—" said Delores.

"Shhh," said Vinny. "Quiet."

I checked the street around us. Nothing. If they were laying for us, it was on the street beyond. They hoped we'd just turn the corner and then they'd shoot us.

Vinny hit the panic button on my key-fob and the car's police lights and horn went off. I turned the corner.

"Police!" I yelled.

I saw a figure in the flash of the lights. It looked to be a man. He raised a hand and I moved as he fired.

I swung into the street and fired the Glock. I saw a spark rise from the street light pole where I'd hit it. I fired the .45 a second later and I heard the slug slam into the concrete of an abandoned house just beyond the car.

I vaguely saw the shooter turn the corner. I started after him, but I wasn't sure he was alone and I had a witness to protect.

"Get to the car!" I said.

Vinny hustled Delores into the car as I covered them. I jumped into the back and we drove away.

I wanted to go after him but that was a fool's errand. I kept forgetting our killer was probably a cop. His car was close by and he was long gone.

"Oh Jesus," said Delores. "Am I in trouble?"

"Yes," I said. "We all are."

****

We took Delores to my father's house as it was closer. We needed to question her before we turned her over to DeAngela in IAD.

My father, Robert Cavanaugh, is a tough old man who still has a touch of Irish brogue in his voice. He's slowed down in his old age, but once, he was the baddest dude I knew. Now, he was mellow, didn't drink, doted on his grandson and liked to watch police videos on what he called "The Youtube."

And he had a girlfriend, a woman named Sophia Samson who he'd met at mass. Just like the brothers, the Irish pick up women at church.

I told dad about the case. I could trust him and he loved to help out. He still had a keen mind and Vinny and I both valued his counsel.

We all sat at the kitchen table and talked while Sophia made coffee.

"He was so much better than me and his daddy," said Delores. Her eyes were so red, they looked bloody. "So smart and never got into any trouble. I don't know who would ever want to hurt him."

"We need to know how your son contacted you," I said. "We think he might have left you a message."

"I walked out of the halfway house to get high," said Delores, not really hearing the question. "He was mad. My baby was mad at me when he died." She started to cry again.

"Now's the time to get clean," my father said abruptly. "I know you feel bad and all, but your boy ain't coming back. I drank for thirty years before I got sober and when I did, it saved my life. You wanna catch whoever killed your boy, listen to them. They know their stuff. And after you bury your son, me and Sophia can go to see Father Carrin at the church and get you into rehab."

Dad was on a very self-righteous kick since getting clean and I was not going to stop him in this case.

Delores stopped crying. Vinny handed her some tissue. We needed to get to this soon or the woman might just run off and overdose or something else stupid.

"Did Raymond keep a phone or email account in your name?" asked Vinny.

"I hid it," said Delores suddenly. "Raymond gave me a phone, a nice one. He left me messages on it sometimes and I didn't want to sell it. I know myself."

"Where is it?" I asked.

"In my old room at the halfway house," said Delores.

Vinny and I looked at each other at the same time. We were not the only ones who knew that. Whoever had found Delores when we did and taken a shot at us also knew.

Sophia brought the coffee. She was a plump little lady with a head of gray hair.

Delores loaded her coffee with sugar and I saw my father shake his head with pity.

"Where?" I asked. "We searched that room."

"It's in the ceiling in the closet," said Delores. I kept it off so no one would hear it.

"This is very important," I said. "The police are going to talk to you about your son's killers. I don't want you to tell them anything about that phone."

"Okay," said Delores. "But why?"

"Cops can't be trusted now," my father said. "Danny, you and Vinny go get that phone. We'll take her downtown."

"IAD, dad," said Vinny.

"Shit, I hate them," said my father casually.

"Cursing," said Sophia.

"Sorry babe," said dad.

Vinny and I left and went back to Second Chances. The new occupant of Delores' old room was not happy about being awakened so late.

We found the phone right where she said it was. It was in a plastic bag along with some pictures of RaRa as a kid.

This made me a little sad but I didn't say anything about it. I was upset because RaRa was a good kid and now he was gone. All of this was getting kind of personal to me. I wanted to go back to Jimmy's and have another fight.

We took the phone back to our house but we didn't tell anyone in the family what we had found.

Vinny and I connected the phone on her laptop and the phone came up like a drive. It was not locked or coded and so we could see everything on it. There were numerous voice messages, and there, the night of the murder was a message with a video file on it.

I pressed the icon and the video played:

"What the fuck?" said Ivory.

Ivory's face popped up and the words "LIVECHATAPP" appeared in the corner in red. Vinny was visibly struck and covered her mouth to stifle a sob.

"Keep me on the line," said RaRa. "Them muthafuckas be trippin' these days."
"No worries," said Ivory. "I got it."
"Oh, it's your sister's man."

"Naw it ain't him. It's... Look, I'll see you at
what time?"
"Nine, Greektown," said RaRa.
"Cool."

Ivory got out of the car and turned into the glare of
the lights behind her and the video went off but not
before catching a shot of the police cruiser and the
serial number plate in its windshield.

12

ICE BREAKER

Thom Ross felt silly wearing the suit which looked like a uniform. He would never understand why some people were so in love with boating. It was a sign of class and status but these people took the shit way too seriously.

The Annual Winter Cruise was coming to a blessed end. It was on a Luxury Yacht named the *Demetier* which was owned by another of the state's old money families.

They had hired an ice breaker to make sure the river could be navigated and didn't lock them in. The ice was thin and they probably didn't need it, but it was still impressive to see the other ship clear a path.

Thom used to love these events, mingling with the upper class, making them laugh with tales of being middle class. But these days, he was in the dog house with Sandra, which meant he was in the same place with her friends. Motherfuckers all stuck together, he thought.

He would remedy that very soon. Sandra could not avoid him forever and when the time was right, he was going to make everything like it was, then he'd make it better.

He watched Sandra, draped in her fur, laughing and drinking with some other women. She certainly wasn't mourning anymore, he thought sarcastically. She was a good actress and was really doing a good job of hiding her pain. She had lost someone and it had to be killing her. All things in good time, he thought.

Thom checked his watch again. He would have plenty of time to run his errand when they docked. There was always an after affair with press but he was skipping it.

Evan had been the boating enthusiast. Sandra had overcome her fear of sailing after falling overboard and almost drowning when she was twelve. Evan had dove into the water and saved her. The family rumor was her father, Quinn had just watched her and did not move.

It had made the newspapers thanks to Sandra's mother who was the original attention whore.

The *Demetier* rolled into the Grosse Pointe Yacht Club and docked. The Captain gave his yearly boring speech and the well-heeled audience ate it up. Thom took this time to sneak away. He found his car, a white Range Rover and drove back home alone. Sandra could catch a ride with friends.

After he got home, he quickly got out of the monkey suit and into some casual clothes. Normally, he'd take the Range Rover but it was too flashy for where he was headed. Luckily, they'd gotten a Ford truck that would do nicely.

He left the house and saw the guard wave. He knew that guard was cataloguing everyone that came and went but he didn't care. Sandra would never guess what he was up to tonight.

He drove to his office at 1 Woodward in downtown Detroit and was let in by the night guard. Thom went to his little suite, an office that was all his and that only he had access to. He entered and then went to the safe he'd put into his desk.

Earlier in the day, he'd gone to his bank and gotten some funds in cash. He removed these funds from his office safe along with the .9mm pistol which he had a license to carry.

He placed the money in an envelope, the gun in a hip holster and then set out.

Thom became nervous as downtown faded away and the dismal grayness of Detroit's east side came into view in the Ford.

He was not born rich, but he had never lived like these people. Houses dotted the landscape and the streets seemed lifeless, like no one lived there. Even though he knew it would all change in a few years, it was still unsettling.

This is why he had gone into business with Renardo. Thom hated these neighborhoods and he didn't much care for the people. They could tell how uncomfortable he was around them and he could barely hide his revulsion at how they lived.

He turned off Davison onto a little street with no sign. He parked near the corner and waited. He sat there a while, checking the time.

Suddenly, two men walked from a house and started up the street his way. These were not his contacts, so he was immediately nervous. He took out the gun and placed it on the seat next to him.

"No problem," he said to himself. "Just keep walking, fellas."

The two men stopped a couple of houses away and looked at his truck which was still running, smoke rising from the exhaust. It was a new vehicle and so if they were thinking anything bad, it had to be carjacking. If he let them, then that was that, he'd be beaten or shot and that was no good. If he shot them then he'd have to run. His mission for tonight would not be completed and that was worse.

When the men started his way again, Thom pulled the truck out and drove down the street away from the men. He checked his rearview mirror as they turned to watch him, then moved on.

Thom parked on a side street and breathed easier. "Damn," he said. "I don't need this shit."

After five minutes, he rounded the corner and parked again where he had been told. After another half hour, he saw a car at the other end of the street. It approached slowly, then passed by him. This was his contact.

The same car came around the corner a few minutes later. This time it stopped. The driver's dark-tinted window rolled down.

Thom handed the envelope to the driver who took the money and counted it quickly.

"How much longer?" asked Thom.

The driver said nothing. The window rolled up and the car took off.

"What the fuck?" said Thom as the car turned the corner.

He was not going to pay any more money until he got some specifics from this asshole. He needed to move on with his life and it was going to be hard enough without all this cloak and dagger bullshit.

Thom cursed again as he pulled away and drove to the boulevard. He saw the two men he had seen earlier. One of them carried a plastic shopping bag.

As he drove by them, the one not carrying a bag threw something and hit the truck. Thom jumped and swerved as the snowball splattered across his windshield.

"Fuck me!" he yelled as he regained control of the truck.

No, he thought as he headed toward the freeway. He did not like these people, not one bit.

13

FAST GIRL

When someone dies, there is a personal reckoning with everyone who knew the deceased. You have to sum up your relationship and filter it down to the bare essence of what it will mean to you.

Ivory Shaw was never good or particularly nice to me and that was what I was left with, memories of an attitude and a side-eye. It was my fault for not correcting it and so I had to live with it forever.

The family was demanding the body for a funeral but I knew it would not be released until we had everything science allowed for evidence.

The snippet of video RaRa sent to his mother had come with a written note that he wanted her to keep it safe for him. He also said that he was not mad at her anymore and that he wanted to get her clean again. This made Delores happy even as she went to identify his body.

The video did not show the officer but we did get a shot of the car from a simple video enhancement that showed the number of the vehicle in the window. But when we went to check to see who that car had been given to that night, the logs showed that no one had it. Again, we were dealing with a pro.

The four officers who were on the street that night, Chance Whitehall, Jacob Vilatinni, Jamilla Cole and Dobbs Harson were registered to other cars. The system for registering cars at the 11th was an out-dated one. The cars had computerized trackers in them and we didn't know if they, or one of the other officers had switched the computer registration card.

When we checked the tracker number it was verified that the cruiser had not left the impound that night. Again, our killer was a cop and would know how to do that.

And something else was in my head:

> *"Oh, it's your sister's man."*
> *"Naw it ain't him. It's…"*

Ivory knew him. She did not say his name but she was not sweating the police stop because it was her man. The cruiser's lights had not been turned on, so it wasn't being done by the book. I was also disturbed by the unstated reference to me, *"Your sister's man."* Obviously, Ivory talked about me with her friends.

I still liked Cole and Harson for it. Something had fractured their relationship and a murder was the kind of thing that would do it.

I went back to see DeAngela. She was not happy and I wasn't either. We were being played like chumps so far and time was not on our side.

"So, a fuckin' ghost killed the girl?" said DeAngela as we sat in her office.

"No, they just swapped the trackers," I said. "Remember, these are cops."

"Any chance he touched the computer when he swapped it?" she asked

"We can dust for fingerprints but I'm thinking he'd be a fool to have done that," I said. "What I want to know is, who took a shot at me when all of the suspects are under surveillance."

DeAngela looked away when I said this and I knew there was bad news on this front.

"I'm sorry about that," said DeAngela. "The city would not sign off on the time I asked for full surveillance and so the teams have been rotating on the suspects."

"You could have told me that before I had to start dodging bullets. So, given that and the fact that a cop could probably elude them anyway, it could have been any of them."

I made a mental note to get RaRa's time of death and check it against whatever log the IAD team had. But I already knew that whoever killed him, had taken him the same night of Ivory's murder. That's what I would have done.

"All we have is that baby," said DeAngela, "because I know the victim's cell phones have been destroyed. I think we should indict all eight of them, then do DNA on the men."

"I'm with that," I said. "Is the prosecutor?"

"You heard Jesse. He doesn't want to blow it on a technicality, but the public and our bosses won't stand for much more."

"The politics of this ain't never been good for us," I said. "No matter what we do, we're gonna catch some kind of hell."

"My bosses are pressing me hard. I'm meeting with the Black Lives Matter people this afternoon. They want to help in any way they can."

"I'd watch it with them," I said. "Their cause is good but they have no regard for who they trample on. They are fighting a much bigger war."

"Thank you for being so concerned about me," said DeAngela.

"Just being a good partner. Don't get excited."

"You'll be happy to know that I picked up a new fella. So you're off the hook—- for now."

"Lucky man," I said. "Anybody I know?"

"Yes, as a matter of fact. Your old boss, James Cole, the Deputy Chief."

"A good man," I said.

Jim Cole was a notorious playboy and had quite a reputation with the ladies.

"I know all about his rep," said DeAngela sensing my mood. "Believe me, it's well-earned."

****

I left IAD and made my way over to Fiona's. She had texted me to come by at lunch time to meet her boyfriend. I dreaded this but I wanted to get a preview of whatever she was going to send to DeAngela on RaRa.

When I arrived, I was greeted by Fiona with a smile, something that I rarely saw. Standing next to her, was a man about forty wearing a very nice suit. He was mixed race, black and Asian, I thought.

"Danny, this is Ngo McDougall," said Fiona.

"Hey," I said and we shook hands.

"I know. I've got some name," said Ngo.

"I like the Irish part of it," I said.

"My father's side," said Ngo. "Mom's Vietnamese. It was an Army thing."

"Danny's a full-blooded Mick," said Fiona.

"Guilty," I said. "So, what do you do in this godforsaken town?"

"I'm a funeral director," he said. "But my company does virtual funerals."

"Do I have to ask?" I said.

"It's pretty cool," said Fiona. "A lot of people don't like funerals and sometimes people die and their relatives can't attend because they are so far away. Ngo can do services in real time and transmit them interpreted anywhere."

"Did you two meet on some kind of death dating site?" I asked jokingly.

"Kind of," said Ngo. "Match.com puts you together based on a lot of shared likes. We are both interested in forensic science."

I liked him. He was very calm and focused on Fiona and I wasn't getting any sinister vibes from him. He probably had an ex wife and kids at his age, but I'm sure Fiona knew that already.

"Ngo, can you excuse us?" asked Fiona. "I have some info for smart boy here."

"No problem Fi," said Ngo. "I can wait outside for you."

Ngo said goodbye and left. I turned to Fiona.

"I don't hate him," I said.

"Don't patronize me," said Fiona.

"How long was he married?" I asked.

"Six years," said Fiona. "He's got a daughter, Tiana. She's five and adorable."

"You ready for that, stepmom?" I asked.

"No," said Fiona, "but I guess I'll have to be. Okay, this is good. I guess we can get to the next stage of our relationship now."

"Wait, you haven't had sex with this guy?" I asked with more than a little shock in my voice.

"I was waiting, to be sure, you know and I had some other issues in that area."

"Issues? Like what?"

"Like it's none of your damned business," said Fiona.

Fiona was almost forty years old but she'd all but told me she was not sexually experienced, or worse, a virgin. How could I have not seen that? She was a nerd and probably some kind of genius and so she was much younger than her peers but I just assumed that she had the normal experiences.

"Just be careful," I said.

"I will," said Fiona, smiling. "So, there is a heart under all that beef. Okay, let's get to business."

"What do you have for me?" I asked, grateful to be moving on.

"Well, they can have her body," said Fiona. "In fact, it can be in transit tomorrow. I have all the DNA on her and the baby and I am ready for matching."

"So, the fetus, where does it go?"

"That's a good question," said Fiona. "Technically, the state does not consider it to be a person and so it's residual matter and we own it."

"Bullshit," I said. "That baby belongs to the family. If they have to live with the pain of it being gone, then they have the right to bury it with its mother."

"I have to make a request," said Fiona.

"Fine but don't send the body without the fetus. I don't want the family to have any more casualties, like heart attacks. We get anything from RaRa's body and his place?"

"No, whoever your boy is, he is good. They wore gloves and probably plastic on his feet. We have prints but they belong to both of the victims. I take it they were dating."

"Yes, they had a thing. But we're betting it was not his baby."

"Raymond was tortured," said Fiona. "He was beaten with a blunt instrument and his fingers were broken with a pair of household pliers, I'm guessing. He had multiple contusions on the face and in the end, he was suffocated."

I was trying my best to stay calm. This killer was brutal and so whatever I was chasing had to be bad.

People kill for all kinds of dumbass reasons, but the extremes in this case were worrying me.

"Do you have a time of death on Raymond?" I asked.

"It's hard given the exposure but near as I can figure he was killed about twelve to twenty hours after the girl."

"I thought so," I said. "Okay, I'll get a copy of whatever you give IAD. Thanks."

"I'm sorry about getting upset," said Fiona. "I'm just nervous about Ngo."

"It's okay. I'm not trippin'. I'm a little on edge, too. Look, I don't know a lot about relationships. I kinda stumble-fucked my way into a good one, you know."

"Everybody knows that," said Fiona smiling.

"Anyway," I said. "I do know this, just be honest and don't change yourself. If he's good, he'll like you for that."

"Got it," said Fiona. "Okay, we're going to lunch. How do I look?"

"Pale and beautiful," I said.

I did my sneaky exit out the back way. I was getting back to my car, when I got a text message from Vinny:

> Marcus Jr. and Ivanna are on
> TV with the black lives matter
> people! I'm gonna kill them!

I sighed heavily and then I got to a TV as soon as I could. Luckily, the guys at the Sewer were already watching the event. I waited and then repeated the broadcast on the DVR.

Marcus Jr. and Ivanna had gone against their mother, father and the family and stood with the Black Lives Matter people at a rally at City Hall. Vinny had told them to keep lines of communication open, but they had taken it further.

The leaders preached to the crowd, keeping their energy high. Pictures of past victims floated above the horde on signs and there was one of Ivory which stood with them like a ghost.

Marcus Jr. gave a speech that was very powerful for someone his age but it was Ivanna who stood there, wearing the face of her dead sister who brought the house down with a tearful plea for action and justice:

> *"My sister has been part of me*
> *since I was just a few cells in my*
> *mother's womb. And all through my*
> *life, I have been dressing like her,*
> *talking like her and been mistaken*
> *for her. I have to look into her face*
> *for the rest of my life because we*
> *look alike. To say I feel like half*
> *of me is gone is not enough. Part of me*
> *was murdered in that police cell and*
> *I die a little every day knowing that it*
> *doesn't matter to many people who*
> *discount millions of us because just*
> *like my sister and I, we look alike."*

The family would punish them, but I could tell that Ivanna and Marcus Jr. didn't care. They'd had enough and wanted to do something to avenge their sister. This was all they had available.

I was kinda proud of them for what they did, especially Ivanna, even though I would have to act like I wasn't.

As much as I have been around black people, I have never felt the weight of what they feel to be discounted by society. It is one thing to face the dangers of the world each day. It's another to do so devalued by people who are authorized to use deadly force.

All cops are biased against anyone who is not white, wealthy or famous. And if they tell you otherwise, what they really mean is, they temper their bias with reason. And when reason isn't enough, people die.

The woman I love, my son and my best friend are all black and yet when I see three young black men congregating, my spider sense goes off, and try as I might, I cannot stop feeling that way.

And my nightmare is that one day, I will have only a second to act and I will choose wrong based on my bias and my soul will go straight to hell, or worse, that decision will be in the hands of some other cop and someone I love will be on the other end of the gun.

I got another text message an hour later, this time from DeAngela and Jesse King. The political and media pressure was too much.

They were also going to release the news that a second victim had been found. RaRa.'s death could not be covered up much longer and the city wanted to get out ahead of the information.

Two unarmed black kids killed by the same cop meant more heat and more trouble. Some of the suspect cops were black but that would make no difference to the media or the movement. Anyone with a badge was one of *them* and immediately suspect.

They were going to indict all of the cops on a variety of charges and then hope one of them would crack.

I called Vinny and told her what I was about to do and she agreed and then cautioned me to be careful.

I was only going to have one shot at making sure our killer did not escape or get himself killed in the process.

I walked out of the Sewer knowing that if I failed, I might not ever be coming back.

14

FLIGHT

Officer Dobbs Harson lined up each of his guns on the kitchen table in the back of his house. When they came, he would fight and go out like a goddamned man.

He had four .9mm handguns, a Glock 18 auto pistol, a Mossberg 500 shotgun, and an AR-15, his pride and joy. More than enough firepower for a real standoff.

"Let them come," he said to himself.

He was already up on speed and he was drinking Jack Daniels straight out of a bottle, rocket fuel, he thought.

He'd considered running, but where would he go? He was fucked and if they wanted it this way, then so be it.

His wife, Glenda and his daughter, Janis would be very disappointed in him, but they didn't understand what he had been through.

They were visiting Glenda's bitch sister, Theresa and they'd be watching on TV. He wished Theresa were here. He'd put one right in her fat fuckin' forehead.

Ivory Shaw had been too tempting for him or any real man. She'd pursued him, sent him naked pictures and sexy text messages. She'd even masturbated on camera once and sent it to him. What the fuck was he supposed to do about that?

She was the most beautiful woman he'd ever been with and she'd really strung him out in the bedroom. He needed it and she knew he was hooked. That's when things started to get ugly.

Ivory said that she just wanted to have fun. Just sex. Sure, she asked for money now and then but they all did. But after a while, she *demanded* everything and if he refused, she'd threaten him.

Dobbs had never been faithful, not even for a year after his marriage. He liked women and he couldn't kick it. And when you're a cop, a lot of women come on to you. It was a toxic mix for him, a blessing and a curse.

But he had tried to settle down with Glenda. She was just the kind of girl he was supposed to marry. Glenda with her good cooking, reasonable sex and toothy blowjobs. In the end, it just didn't take.

Ivory was what he needed. Shit, she was what every man needed. She was beautiful and adventurous. She liked hard sex, hair pulling, ass-slapping and dirty talk. All the stuff respectable women didn't do.

Why did she have to go and get pregnant on him? Just a few times he slipped up and released inside her. She got knocked up and then wanted to keep it.

And then Jamilla, that traitorous bitch. She had cut a deal with Jesse King behind his back. She talked with them then tried to say that nothing had been said. That was some bullshit. They had offered her a deal. She'd thought about it, then she took it and now they were coming to get him.

"Fucking bitch!" he yelled to no one. "Disloyal fucking bitch!"

Thank God their source in the prosecutor's office had tipped them all that it was coming. But he did not wait quietly like a pussy. No, he was going to roar so loudly, that no one would forget it.

Everything was going wrong, he thought in his fevered mind. Marriage crumbling, job gone and now, prison. He'd never last. He'd rather go out like this, a blaze of glory, like that cop in Los Angeles.

Dobbs picked up the AR-15 and checked it as the first police sirens sounded in the distance.

"Let's rock, motherfuckers," he said. "Let's rock."

****

Dr. Sandra Bell-Ross rushed to her car outside of the small building in Grosse Pointe Park. It was chilly and she was still hot from the yoga session. She wanted to get home and get into a hot shower and watch some TV.

She loved to watch medical shows and laugh at the doctors as they said and did things that would kill their patients in real life.

She threw her bag onto the front seat and climbed in the big Mercedes S. She turned the car over and pulled off into traffic. There was still a lot of moisture on the road and so she drove slowly.

She jerked the wheel when she saw the shadowy figure in her backseat.

"Oh, God!" she exclaimed as she swerved in traffic.

"Calm your ass down," said Renardo from the backseat. "Just keep driving and nothing's gonna happen, lady."

He showed her a gun. He tried to disguise his voice and he wore a black ski mask. He felt silly but this was necessary for now.

"You can have my money and the car," said Dr. Ross. "Just don't—"

"Shut the fuck up, please," said Renardo. "Head up this street and keep them hands on the wheel. And give me your phone."

She started to cry and Renardo knew he was going to have to take action. This dumb bitch would crash the car and then he'd be fucked. He took her phone, then tossed it out the window.

He'd paid a lot of money for the car code replicator he borrowed from his friend who was a high-end car thief. That's how he had gotten in but he didn't think she would go to pieces so quickly.

"Pull the car over, in that alley, now," he said.

Dr. Ross did and Renardo got out and forced her into the trunk of his own car which had been left there.

He tied her hands and feet and then stuffed her scarf into her mouth and put a sack on her head. He tossed her purse and then got back into his car.

"Damn females," he said.

He drove into the city into a desolate part of town. He pulled into an old plant he and Kelvin sometimes used then they needed to get things done in secret.

Kelvin waited but he did not look happy. He ran over to his boss and together they removed Dr. Ross who was shaking and took her into the room they had prepared for her. It had a bathroom, a space heater and a cot. They sat her down in a chair.

"Don't move lady," said Renardo.

She just sobbed and slumped in the chair as they walked out of the room.

In the larger space, Renardo and Kelvin walked away from the room. Renardo took out his cell phone and turned on a program. The doctor popped up on his screen from the camera they had placed in the room with her.

"Good," he said.

"Hope we don't have to kill this bitch," said Kelvin.

"That's up to Thom," said Renardo. "If we do, then he's fucked. He said once that his wife's family had him cut out of the money. If that's true and she dies, he's broke. He'll pay for that."

"So we call him and ask for money?"

"Oh no. I'm gonna do this in person," said Renardo.

****

"Officer Harson, this is the police and the FBI! Come out and surrender to custody!"

I could hear them clearly from Dobbs' little basement where I had been hiding for hours now. I'd broken into

Dobbs' house while he was out buying liquor and drugs for his siege.

I knew all the officers would find out about the indictments. Information like that was hard to keep secret and the cops had many friends in the county prosecutor's office.

Dobbs was just Ivory's type, like Bakersfield. Very handsome, dangerous and no good. He also had a reputation as a playboy and was a gun nut. Dobbs bragged about his high-powered weapons and did survival training. This was why I knew I had to intercede. Guys like that never went quietly.

Dobbs had knocked up Ivory and when she tried to force him to pay her for an abortion or worse, force him into fatherhood, he'd lost it and killed her.

Jamilla covered for him but in the end, there was too much heat.

So, I'd taken a chance and broke into his house before the news got out and sure enough, he came home and armed himself. I could hear him talking to himself very loudly as he stomped around and I heard the sound of guns being loaded.

I would have taken him sooner but I didn't want gunplay. One of us would end up dead. When the cops came, he'd be distracted and I'd sneak up on him.

Dobbs helped me out when he started playing loud rock music. He was getting himself ready to do some damage and the music would be a good cover for me. He played U2. I hated U2.

I flexed an arm upwards. The Kevlar vest I wore was uncomfortable. Normally, I would not have worn one. I told myself it was because Dobbs was well-armed but I was thinking about my family. I admit it, I was being cautious now.

"Officer Harson, we do not want an altercation. Please come out with your hands in the air."

It was hard to hear over the music but it was a second warning. One more and they would storm the place.

I started walking up the creaking wooden stairs in his basement. My heart rate was going up but I did not pull a weapon. If I was good, there would be no need to. If not, then one of us would be going out in a bag.

I got to the top of the stairs and pushed the door open a little. The kitchen was empty and there were guns on the table, a lot of them.

I opened the door and walked into the little kitchen. I moved to the door that led from the kitchen to the dining area. I was about the peek inside to see where Dobbs was, when the door opened and the long barrel of a rifle appeared.

****

Renardo waited for Thom in the little waffle house in Plymouth. He'd worn a nice suit and had brought a gun with him just in case. Kelvin was watching the woman back at the place and so far, it was all good.

On the news, the police had arrested eight cops in the death of that black girl. That was some shit, Renardo thought. Arrogant motherfuckers, killing a girl in a police precinct. But these days, he put nothing past them. He'd never liked the cops and now everyone was seeing what they were.

They had surrounded the house of one of them. He was holed up and the news reported that this cop was known to have high-powered guns. There was probably going to be a shootout.

Renardo hoped they'd do all of society a favor and kill each other.

Thom entered about a half hour after Renardo sat down. He made his way to the back of the place and sat across from the black man.

"All hell's breaking loose in Detroit," said Thom. "Jesus. So, what's so important that you drag me out here and don't say I did it first."

"It's about that thing," said Renardo, "the end of our business dealings."

"What about it?" said Thom. "I hope you don't want more because I'll walk right out of here."

"I got your wife."

This silenced Thom whose eyes started to widen. He searched Renardo's face for humor or a bluff but found none.

"What kind of goddamned shit is this?" Thom Ross said.

"Two million and you can have her back," said Renardo.

"What? No way. Kill the bitch. I don't care."

"Cool," said Renardo as he whipped out his phone.

"Goddammit, wait!" Thom said in a hushed voice. "Look, you don't know what you've done. This is a federal crime. If I report it—"

"Right," said Renardo. "Poor dumb Renardo is gonna be scared of the feds. Man, that's just a better prison to go into. I want my fucking money, what was promised to me. And this will do it or I'ma kill that bitch and you will get nothing. And after I do her, I'm coming after you."

"Look, she... her family controls the money. I could get it but I need her to do it," Thom looked scared for the first time.

"How do they keep control of the money?" asked Renardo.

"You wouldn't understand," said Thom. "It's lawyer shit."

"Try me," said Renardo. "I'm smart, remember?"

"The money passes on her side of the family," said Thom. "She dies and the trust shuts me out. I get nothing, you get nothing."

"You got a week to get my money or I start scattering the doctor all over the city," said Renardo.

"How do I know she's not already dead?"

Renardo dialed his cell then held it out for Thom to listen. He heard Kelvin instruct his wife to say something. She cried and said her name. Thom's expression never changed.

"Happy?" asked Renardo. He hung up the call.

"I'll need ten days for the money," said Thom flatly. "Have to sell some things. Then we'll work it out."

"Okay," said Renardo. "And oh yeah, if you try any funny shit like fake money or if you go to the police, just know that I'm ready to go all the way."

"Remember what I said about you not being a nigger?" said Thom getting up.

"Yeah, you was wrong about that," said Renardo. "I'm all nigga and we don't ever trust white people. Believe that."

Thom muttered a curse then walked out, his feet hitting the floor heavily.

Renardo was about to go, when he realized that he had not eaten in a long time. He grabbed a menu and signaled to a waitress.

****

Adrenalin shot into my system as the barrel of the AR-15 came through the door. I waited until I saw Dobbs' hand and then I made my move.

I grabbed the gun where his hand was and shot an elbow up into his chin.

Dobbs fell back into the other room and I had the gun. I tossed it into the kitchen and fell on Dobbs who was regaining his footing.

He reached for one of two guns he had on his hip and I caught his hand as he grabbed it and turned it away from me. We struggled for it and I saw recognition flash in his eyes.

With my free hand, I hit him in the gut and he doubled over.

The gun fired out the window.

I grabbed Dobbs and pulled him to the floor hard and a second later, the place was hit with gunfire. The window exploded inward and we were both showered with glass.

On the floor, we wrestled and I easily won as he was high and I had surprised him. I disarmed him and turned him over as debris fell all over the place and guns thundered outside.

I pulled Dobbs into the kitchen and handcuffed him. I sat on his back as I pulled out my cell and dialed.

In the other room, a tear gas canister flew inside and went off.

"DeAngela! It's Danny Cavanaugh. Are you outside of Dobbs' house?"

"Danny?" said DeAngela. "Yes, I'm here. He shot at us. The police are about to storm him. Where are you?"

"I'm inside with Dobbs! Tell them to stop firing!"

"What, how did you—"

"Just tell them to stop before they kill both of us!"

The shooting stopped a long minute later. Something in Dobbs' other room fell and hit the floor hard.

"Danny?" said DeAngela.

"I'm here. I got him," I said.

Dobbs was crying beneath me and squirming like a baby. I hit him in the head and it felt good.

"Shut the fuck up," I said.

"I didn't do it!" Dobbs cried. "I swear!"

"Of course you didn't," I said, surprised at how angry I was. "DeAngela, I want you to come in and we'll walk him out together." I coughed as the gas wafted into the kitchen.

"They won't let me do that," she sounded afraid.

"You said you wanted credit, this is it. I walk him out alone, and I have a lot of explaining to do. Tell them to send a couple of cops with you."

"Okay, I'll try."

We hung up and five minutes later, officers bashed in the front door. DeAngela entered with three tactical officers.

I held Dobbs up by his cuffs and handed him over to the police officers. By now, both of us were choking and our eyes were red from the gas.

"Jesus Christ, Cavanaugh," said one of the officers who I knew. "You sure got a way of staying in trouble, man."

"Tell me about it," I said.

After reading him his rights, we walked Dobbs out of his house. The street was lined with police vehicles, ambulances, fire trucks and armed officers. Their guns were lowered but the cops stood at the ready as the suspect walked by.

Most of the cops looked sad and disappointed but a few had stone cold hatred in their eyes. Not for me, but for Dobbs. Anyone knew, when you ran, you were guilty.

The media had been moved off but their cameras caught it all. Dobbs lowered his head to avoid being recorded.

I looked away from the cameras as well but DeAngela made sure they saw the steely determined look on her face. High heels and a bullet proof vest would be the headline the next day.

I heard a distant cheer and I saw the Black Lives Matter people had been allowed to gather further up the street away from the media.

Dobbs was taken into custody. I avoided all of the press by hitching a ride with a cruiser that was nearby. My car was several blocks over and they took me to it.

After I got inside my car, my first call was to my boss. I told Erik what went down. He was happy about it and agreed to spin it my way with his bosses.

My second call was home. The family was gathered at my house again and I presumed Vinny had told them my plan had been successful.

"Hey, we got him alive," I said. "I got some stuff to do, then I'm on my way."

15

STATE PROPERTY

It was a good day for the police. We had taken down a rotten apple and the world watched us do it. Everyone in the city government was either spinning or taking credit.

My name was being mentioned quite a bit but I didn't keep track. I was proud of what I had done but I knew that if I had screwed it up, everyone would be throwing me under the nearest bus and disavowing my actions.

Dobbs Harson was under suicide watch. He'd been processed and seen by a doctor who'd made the ruling.

Dobbs had cried the whole time and insisted that he was innocent, until his lawyer had come in and told him to shut up.

Dobbs' wife was in the hospital having fainted when she heard the news of his arrest. Their kid was safe with relatives but sooner or later, she would know what happened.

Police found twenty-three weapons in Dobbs' house and enough ammo to hold off an army. I don't believe in gun control but, I'm pretty sure the Constitution didn't grant gun rights for craziness like that.

Dobbs would have been killed for sure but there was no telling how many cops he would have taken with him.

Jamilla Cole and the other officers had been processed and had all made bail, a fact that had angered many people in the activist community. But Dobbs was not going to be granted that favor as he was now a flight risk. That would quiet them down, I hoped.

I was greeted to a hero's welcome at my house and I had to chase Lenny, my neighbor away. The media was back, sneaking around again and this time, I could not avoid them. Vinny called some cops and soon even they were gone.

Renitta, the oldest sister in the clan had bear hugged me and I knew it was hard for her given her historic contempt for me. Vinny's mother, Cassandra, had kissed me several times through her tears.

I took it all in stride and even managed a half smile. In truth, I was dog ass tired. I went straight into my son's room and kissed him while he slept. I stood there a moment, with a lot of stuff running through me some good some not so good. Life was what it was, I concluded and there was nothing I could do about it.

Ivanna and Marcus Sr. came in after I got there and it was not pretty. Although the family was happy about the arrest, they were pissed that the kids had gone rogue.

Actually, they were split right down age lines, the older ones were upset but the younger ones understood why they had done it. In the end, they were all willing to forgive. There had been enough tragedy and they had to put their sister to rest.

Vinny and I decided to talk to her mother and father about Ivory first. We told them all of the gory details. They were hit hard but now that we had a suspect, they accepted it. From there, we told the rest of the family.

"Do they know the sex of the baby?" asked Vinny's mother who had started crying.

"No," I said. "Too early to tell, really."

"We want the baby to bury with its mother," said Marcus Sr.

"I'm working on it, sir," I said. "The state doesn't consider the baby to be… I'll get it done."

"The state doesn't think it's human," said Juan. "They take the cells from it and then sell them."

"That's not true," said Easter. She was usually quiet but she was a dentist, essentially a doctor and this was something she new about. "They don't do that when there's a mother."

"This is important," said Marcus Sr. "The world is watching and we can help people see once and for all, that a fetus is a life made by God and should be respected."

Marcus Sr.'s voice had gone into that resonant cadence preachers get when they are serious. Everyone became silent and I was not about to be the one to go against him on this.

"We'll get the kid," said Vinny. "Don't worry."

The rest of the night was a blur. There was food and discussion and I was forced to tell the story about Dobbs. After a couple of beers, I was out.

I know I dreamed about something but it wasn't good and I can't exactly remember what it was.

I woke up the next morning to a quiet house. I savored it for a while and then set out early to end Every Wadson's murder case. I had been thinking about it for a while and I had a solution.

The media was out again and caught me going to my car.

"Are you a hero?" yelled one reporter.

"How did you get into the house? Who fired the shot at police?" asked another.

I ignored them and resisted the temptation to give them the finger as I drove away.

I checked my messages and I had one from Jimmy, the Samoan. He said he wasn't in trouble but wanted to talk to me. I made a mental note to call him back.

Later, I sat with John Long at his house and told him that because no one was there except him and the deceased, that it was probably a case of self-defense and he had been too afraid to say anything for fear of the drug suppliers. He readily agreed and turned himself in.

With the media turned to Dobbs Harson's capture and after a call to Jesse King, John Long would be back at his business before the dinner rush.

I walked into The Sewer later that day a little worried that my peers had judged me for taking down one of our own. Cops are funny like that. Dobbs was dirty but I had stepped out of my place.

There was no applause but the guys were generally complimentary to me. There were several who just muttered "Good job" and one who said nothing and avoided me. All in all, not bad.

Erik damned near hugged me when we were alone. He had been called by the mayor, Chief Hill and the City Council Chief and congratulated. The official story was the Sewer and IAD had done it together. Cops working to preserve their reputation. The newspapers ate it up.

"You are a crazy ass sonofabitch," said Erik. "I didn't think we'd take Dobbs alive. When I heard tactical was called, I figured his ass was toast."

"Got lucky," I said. "I heard DeAngela has been all over the national news this morning."

"I don't think that woman ever went to bed," said Erik. "Look, if you want to take a few days for the funeral and all, I got you covered."

"Thanks," I said. "I think I will. The family is pretty messed up and there are a few complications."

"Dobbs got another lawyer," said Erik. "Willie Backus is going to take it."

"Backus? Big time," I said.

"The other cops were all released. Jamilla's got a guard on her. She had to have covered for him, so she's fucked."

I nodded silently. I knew the mess was just beginning. After a big arrest, the lawyers, the court and now the media and the Internet would weigh in and judge. It was likely that Dobbs could never receive a fair trial anywhere in the country now.

I closed out the Wadson murder, doing all the paperwork, which would find John Long on probation and a hero in his neighborhood. Just like we agreed, there were complaints about me in the file which had been sent to Erik.

I ignored the many calls to the office and to my cell for interviews. DeAngela was taking a lot of the pressure off of me by doing so much press. Avoiding them had made me a pretty hot ticket but I was going to wait it out. In time, some actress would get divorced and they would forget about me.

In the meantime, Marcus Jr. and Ivanna had become minor celebrities and their online followers had skyrocketed. I still don't understand that shit. We now worship ordinary people because tragedy has visited them.

When I was done with the volume of paperwork and Erik signed off on it, I rushed over to holding to see how the Dobbs interview was going.

I was now allowed to watch along with the rest of the team. There was some resentment amongst the IAD squad toward me. I had upstaged them I guess and many of them thought I was an out of control cop myself. I had a thick file with them. I couldn't argue about that.

Dobbs looked like shit as he sat with DeAngela, Jesse King and his lawyer, the legendary Willie Backus.

Backus was a king in the criminal defense game. He had been a firebrand civil rights lawyer and had won many landmark cases over the years.

Backus' father, had been one of the first black attorneys in the Midwest, graduating from Harvard then moving to Detroit to represent black folks.

PART ONE: LIFE CITY

Willie Backus sat as a judge briefly but got restless and returned to criminal defense, specializing in white collar crime. Now semi-retired, he only took high profile cases and this fit the bill nicely.

Backus was a smallish, dark-skinned man with a bald head and a gray goatee. He wore thick glasses and had a bit of a southern accent like many of the older blacks in the city.

DeAngela had almost knelt to Backus when he walked in. Of course Backus was connected in politics and DeAngela was thinking about the future.

Jesse King wasn't impressed by Backus and even managed to be a little dismissive. It was all war with him. I liked that.

"After talking with my client extensively," Backus began, "we are pleading not guilty. Our defense is he didn't do it."

"Okay," said Jesse. "Duly noted. Then this will be a short interview."

"My client admits to an affair with the deceased. He admits they argued about the baby and he admits he had sex with her the night of the murder but he did not kill her nor did he or his partner bring the deceased into the 11th Precinct."

"That's a lot of admissions," said DeAngela.

"None of it is illegal," said Jesse. "He's saying this is a mistake, correct?"

"That's for you to prove," said Backus.

"What about the missing surveillance?" asked Jesse.

"The system malfunctioned," said Backus. "All of the records will prove that it was offline due to a malfunctioning junction box."

"Does he admit to switching out the police cruiser ID's?" asked Jesse. "Or did that just happen by itself?"

Backus looked at Dobbs, then whispered to him. Dobbs said something back frantically.

"He does not," said Backus. "You'll have to prove that too, if you can."

"This is silly," said Jesse King. "We have DNA, witnesses, flight and a televised stand off. Willie, I know you are great but you can't win. Save us all some aggravation and we can place your client where he will be safe."

"I've been around a long time, Mr. King and like you I know the game, hell some say I invented it. I would normally tell my client to give in but there's just one thing. I believe him and I am not about to go against forty years of gut instinct just because you're the current bright boy."

"If we go through a long trial, I can assure you that I will get the max on him for everything and I will make sure he goes into a hell hole," said Jesse.

"Maybe your boss will be more reasonable. I'll just call her when this is over," said Backus.

"*This* is not some preliminary," said Jesse. "And if you try to go over my head, all you'll find is the sky."

DeAngela looked a little upset at this. These two men were seriously threatening each other now and she didn't like it.

"Guys there's no need for this," said DeAngela. "We got it Willie, you intend to fight and we intend to bring our case."

"Ah, the cool head of a woman," said Backus. "You are right, Ms. Gomez. Mr. King, I apologize for my manner. Let's discuss discovery and all the tedious stuff, shall we?"

"Yes, we can do that but for now, your client has to go back to his cell," said Jesse.

"Can we take him off suicide watch?" asked Backus. "That kind of thing is very prejudicial."

"Sorry," said Jesse. "No can do. Doctor's orders."

Suddenly, the door to the observation room opened and Fiona walked in. Fiona to my knowledge, had never come to a precinct house.

For a second, I thought there was trouble with Ngo, that something had gone wrong but her face did not say that.

"Fiona?" I said.

"Hey," said Fiona. "I was hoping to find you here. We need to talk now."

We moved to the hallway as the IAD cops watched us go. I was kind of glad to be out of the room.

"Lovely crowd you hang with," said Fiona. In her hands, I saw she had a sealed report.

"So, what's up?" I asked.

Fiona took in a deep breath and then: "We ran Dobbs Harson's DNA against the fetus and it doesn't match."

A long moment passed and I swear, I heard these fatal words in sluggish, slow syllables. This was our only theory, our ace in the hole and now it was gone.

"You have got to be shitting me." I said. "Any chance it's a mistake?"

"No," said Fiona. "We rushed the test but then we took our time with the FBI the second and third times. He is *not* the father as they say."

"Okay, so maybe Dobbs just thought it was his baby and he killed her. That can still be—"

"The baby isn't Ivory Shaw's either," said Fiona cutting me off. "We did a match on the mother as a matter of course and it came back negative every time."

I had a strong urge to sit down and bury my head. I was shocked beyond my own cynical belief.

"A surrogate," I almost whispered.

"I'm afraid so," said Fiona.

The money, I thought. That's where Ivory had gotten all that money from.

I stood there with Fiona knowing that this information would make the already sensational case even more so. And I realized that my work, which had been stressful and dangerous, was not close to being done.

PART THREE:

GRIND CITY

"I'm in transition… like the universe."

- Impala

16

HOMEGOING

In a traditional Irish funeral, a window is opened to allow the spirit of the deceased to leave the house, no-one must stand or block the path to the window because this could prevent the spirit from leaving and bring misfortune to the person who blocks their route. After two hours, the window would be closed to prevent the spirit from returning.

This little myth was in the back of my mind as I sat on the hard wooden pew at the Church of God in Christ between Vinny and my father.

Ivory's body had been kept in a locked room in a meat freezer for a long time and I wondered if her spirit was restless.

I didn't know about the open window but for me Ivory's spirit would never rest until we caught the people who killed her, because while Dobbs Harson was a crazy lowlife bent cop, I wasn't sure he killed her anymore.

Ivory had been carrying a surrogate baby and there were lots of places it could have been implanted. Surrogates get paid money but why didn't Ivory tell her family or friends what she was doing? Was this off the books and who would need something like that and why?

One thing was sure, I was looking for a doctor or doctors connected to this. Fiona had given me a list of doctors and facilities in the metro area that specialized in fertility. I would be paying a visit to one of them very soon.

My first thought was Bakersfield, but he was a heart specialist by trade and he and Ivory were at odds. Still, he was a doctor and so he was first on my list.

Winter had come to the city with serious intention. Cold winds from Canada with some of that goddamned arctic air swept into town and froze everything. The river iced over and the roads were very dangerous until the salt trucks got out.

The only hot thing in the city was the murder case against Dobbs Harson and his partner who was charged as an accessory. The other six cops were all charged with dereliction, obstruction and petty stuff and all of it would be dropped when no one was looking.

Every major news outlet had led with the story and there was a rumored bidding war for an interview with Dobbs Harson and Jamilla. That made me a little sick but I understood it.

It would be like Willie Backus to let Dobbs talk to the public, to sway any potential jurors.

We are so obsessed with money and fame that a murderer is now considered a celebrity. I know this is nothing new, but the intensity we level upon them now unsettles me. It's almost like we admire them for what they did, like we're all regressing back to the animals we used to be, when the biggest and baddest ruled by might.

I'm old enough to remember when people didn't want to know about killers or which celebrity did whatever in their bedroom. But I am young enough to know that this is a natural evolution and it will not change and one day we may have live executions or a real Hunger Games.

Ivory's funeral was standing room only. She had a lot of friends and her family attended church there, but many of the people here were just busy-bodies and I was sure there were reporters in the crowd.

No cameras were allowed and one man had already been removed for trying to take video.

Marcus Sr. had been planning the funeral for weeks, so when her body was released, he sent the word out, not wanting to wait.

Fiona, DeAngela, Jesse King and I were the only ones who knew about the baby. We were going to sit on the information for as long as we could. Backus assumed the test was positive and so he would not be asking for a while.

This meant Dobbs Harson thought it was his baby, too. It didn't mean he was innocent and so I felt no guilt about it.

I couldn't tell all of the family about the baby and so we just told the mom and dad. I knew I could trust them. They would convince everyone else that we would have to have a separate funeral.

It was very bad to let them live under the belief that the baby was being held by the state but it was necessary. My killer was still out there and I did not want him to have any advantage.

The funeral was a sad and tearful event and I dreaded my turn to address the crowd because I didn't know what to say about a girl like Ivory. But after all the singing and praying and crying, it was finally my turn.

Vinny smiled at me holding RMC. I really didn't want him to be at this but he'd never remember it. I got up and walked onto the stage where a full choir, the reverend, the deacons and acolytes sat. I was painfully aware that the acolytes' dresses and I were the only white things on the stage.

"I ain't no good at this," I began. "Y'all know I don't do a lot of talking and well, Ivory never warmed up to me very much. But even knowing that, me and Vinny went out and risked our lives to bring her killer to justice. Truth is, I blame myself for my relationship with Ivory. I never tried to find out why she was so distant and now I have to live with that for the rest of my life. That's on me. But I can say that she was always full of life and willing to help anyone that needed it. She cried when my son was born and so I knew family was important to her. When she took the baby from me I remember her saying, 'He's gonna be a good one, I can feel it.' And she kissed him. That's how I'm gonna remember her."

I was surprised to see people crying at this. I thought I sounded dumb and awkward but I guess we were all worked up now.

"Thanks everybody," I said and I stepped down.

PART THREE: GRIND CITY

These services ended and the outdoor burial was only for family. There was a lot of hand-shaking and hugging and more tears as we made our way out.

I tried to be as warm and accommodating as I could. I was very uncomfortable and my mind was back on the case, so I didn't want people to think that I was not sad about all this. I was just focused.

We all froze our asses off at the graveside ceremony as the body was placed into the cold ground. There's nothing more depressing than the big, dark hole sitting next to the casket. When my time came, I did not want this. Cremate me and scatter me on the river, I thought.

I had heard a lot of spiritual poetry during the day but one thing the Reverend Grant said at the gravesite stuck with me:

> *"Whenever I bury someone this young,*
> *I wonder about God. I wonder about his*
> *wisdom and yes, I wonder if he's real.*
> *Preachers talk about God's mystery and*
> *a lot of it is a dodge, a way to avoid saying*
> *things that are uncomfortable. But I can't*
> *do that. God doesn't take a girl from this life*
> *like this. This is our doing. This is our*
> *Earth, our lives and Free Will. We did*
> *this, all of us. And so let us commend our*
> *sister to the ground and commit ourselves*
> *to making this world better because God*
> *was done with us a long time ago, but we*
> *don't have to be done with him."*

PART THREE: GRIND CITY

A light snow began again as we dropped white roses on the coffin and laid Ivory Shaw to rest for good.

When the final words were said, the family went off to eat and drink, tell funny stories and continue the process of healing from their loss.

On the way to the family gathering, I called back Jimmy the Samoan and got his voicemail. I left a message. I was glad he had not picked up. I didn't need more drama right now.

I got to the party, which was at Vinny's parents' house but I would not stay long. I was going to do my healing in a different way. I had a killer to find and I knew where I was going to start.

PART THREE: GRIND CITY

17

THE DEAL

I stood outside of Jamilla Cole's door for a good ten minutes before she finally opened the door to her place.

I came inside and stomped the snow from my feet as she watched me with an angry look on her face.

Her place was not what I was expecting. Most cops were slobs when they lived alone. Jamilla's place looked like Martha Stewart exploded in it. Everything looked coordinated, clean and neat.

"Well, well, the white/black man comes to visit," said Jamilla.

"Nice place," I said.

She had been drinking and in fact held a glass in her hand filled with liquor.

"I'm a neat freak," she said. "My mama gave it to me. Everybody gets that look on their face when they come in."

She was a full-sized girl with big hips and a tight little afro. She was light brown and had freckles, which stood out on her face like paint.

Jamilla was single and in her early thirties and rumored to be a lesbian. I didn't think so. She liked men but probably had trouble finding and keeping one.

Jamilla had that way about her that some black women had, a tendency to be distant and dismissive of men. Personally, I found that part of their appeal. Nothing good ever comes easy.

"Thanks for letting me in," I said.

"I guess I should be glad you didn't break in and tackle my ass like you did Dobbs. Dumbass. I told him… You know what? I ain't talking to you. Get yo ass out before I call my lawyer and have you arrested."

"I know he didn't do it," I said. "And I know you didn't either. That's why I'm here."

"The fuck you talkin' 'bout? Of course he did it. He was fucking her!" She stopped then walked over to me and patted me down for a wire. "I'm speaking off the record now. If you try to use this against me, it won't fly."

"If I got this right, all you did was look the other way while they had sex. I'm betting you did that a lot with Dobbs."

"Yeah, I did," said Jamilla taking a gulp of her drink. "Man was a freak. Could not keep it in his pants. That young girl had him sprung but you all know that."

"Where did they have sex that night?" I asked.

"No, you got to go!" said Jamilla refilling her drink. "I already said too much. You took down a brother. You can't be trusted no more."

"Someone murdered a girl and framed you," I said. "What about that? Look, if I can get this guy, you can keep your job."

This got her attention. The glazed look in her eyes was gone and she moved closer to me.

"How you figure that, Cavanaugh?" she asked.

"If Dobbs didn't do it, there's no crime to connect you to. He's fucked because he resisted arrest and I'm pretty sure he switched out the computer tracking on the cruisers. You can deny knowing about that."

She was thinking now and I had to close her or she would find a way to shut me out. Truth was, I didn't know if the department would go easy on her or not.

"The bosses won't like you and there will be some people giving you looks," I said, "but in the end, you stood by your partner. Hell, I'd ride with a partner that loyal, wouldn't you?"

"I followed the rules, you know," said Jamilla putting down the drink. "I didn't rat him but he deserved it." She waited a moment and then: "They did it at my place. Dobbs did that a lot, fucked girls at my place. No trace. He uh, he paid me for it some times. Didn't ask where he got the money but you know how that is."

"I do," I said. "Bent a little, bent a lot." What I meant was, that since Dobbs was doing his dirt on company time, that he probably shook down local dealers or was being paid by one. "So, the last time you saw Ivory that night was here by your place?"

"No," said Jamilla. "Dobbs dropped me off at a diner that night. I had some food while they did it. Little ho probably told him about the kid, they argued and then they screwed. They did that a lot, some kind of freaky foreplay."

Her place was not too far from the 11th. I had the feeling they were not there by themselves that night, that Ivory was taken right under their noses by whoever killed her.

"Where's Ivory's car?" I asked. "How'd Dobbs get rid of it?"

"Don't know," said Jamilla. "Dobbs knew where she always parked. After we found her, he was panicked as hell. He must have driven it away after our shift."

"What do you think happened?" I asked eager to hear her version of it.

"I don't even know," said Jamilla. "With the security down and at that time of night, she could've gotten in easily. Me and Dobbs were just hanging out but he did disappear for a while."

I watched her as she took another drink and something occurred to me again. Jamilla was a fairly attractive women but had no man. She was mad at Dobbs but her condemnation of him felt like the kind of anger more fueled by personal disappointment than frustration.

"How long were you and he involved?" I asked.

She was silent for a moment and I could tell she was thinking about lying and then: "Not long," she said. "We hooked up a few times, mostly when we got high together." Then she looked at me and added: "You know how it is."

"Yeah, I do," I said. "We got a baby now."

"I heard. Vinny was smart. She got off the force. Not good for mothering."

"Thanks, Jamilla," I said. "I know this was hard. If you think of anything that can help, let me know."

PART THREE: GRIND CITY

"If Dobbs didn't kill her," said Jamilla, "I'd be shocked. When he talked about her, he was always angry as fuck."

I just nodded then left. I made my way back to the Sewer to talk to Erik. I was going to have to let him in on what I was doing now.

I found him talking with one of the big brass on the Police Commission. He introduced me and I had to tell the Dobbs story again but I had it down by now. When we were alone, I gave Erik the bad news.

"Fuck me ten ways to Sunday," said Erik. "She was incubating someone else's kid?"

"Looks like it unless God is looking to save mankind again," I said.

"Well, this is easy," said Erik. "We find the doctor and we find our killer, right?"

"Maybe. So far, whoever this is has been really smart about it. Somehow, I don't think they left tracks."

"How long is this going to take because I need you back to it. Maybe we let the prosecutor sort it all out," said Erik.

"You wanna tell that to Vinny and her clan for me?" I asked.

"Look, nobody said this shit was gonna be easy, Danny. I'm your friend but I'm your boss, too. I let you do that bullshit murder to get Dobbs but now we got him."

"It's not his baby," I said.

"You think he didn't do it?" said Erik. "Okay, the baby ain't his, but he's still dirty."

"Why kill her in the precinct then? Don't add up. It's got to be one of the other seven. I'm hoping they think they got away with it. And let their guard down."

"All right," said Erik. "I know that tone of voice. You're going to do it no matter what I say. You're gonna take some grief time, so if you screw this up, it's not on me or the department, but you have to do something for it."

"No press," I said way ahead of him.

"Everybody wants to talk to you. I've had it with the silent but strong shit. You ain't Batman, nigga."

I couldn't help but laugh little. Not at the Batman joke but the nigga comment. Erik did love me like a brother.

"What do I have to do?" I asked giving in.

"*Free Press* wants to talk to you as part of a story they're doing about the case. A reporter's gonna call you. Just give him something juicy and we call it even. And after that, I'm sure they will all leave you alone."

"Not holding my breath on that," I said. "Okay, so am I good otherwise?"

"Yeah," said Erik. "But if this info hits the town, I might have to tell you to back off, so you need to get to it quickly."

I left The Sewer feeling upset but Erik was right. I hated the press and I wanted to keep a low profile but people did want to know about this. I justified what I was going to do by saying it was for Ivory.

But first, I called Marcus Sr. and told him and Cassandra that I was going to talk to the local paper. They were all for it surprisingly and I said that I would

PART THREE: GRIND CITY

try not to embarrass the family. They thought that was funny for some reason.

Fiona was waiting for me when I came to her lab to talk. Given the circumstances, she was looking surprisingly well. I immediately thought that she and Ngo had finally hooked up. I knew she'd never tell me and so I took her bright attitude as her statement. I was happy for her. That was at least a little good news on an otherwise shitty day.

Fiona had gathered all of the fertility clinics in the area and cross-referenced against our list of suspects. Nothing connected them to our case.

"Somebody put that baby in there," I said.

I had Fiona look up Bakersfield's medical practice to see if there was a fertility specialist there. There wasn't.

"It can't be a coincidence that Bakersfield is a doctor," I said out loud.

"You're asking the wrong question, smart boy," said Fiona. "I'd be asking why someone would want a secret surrogate baby. Can't figure that one."

"Me neither. Ivory had a whole other life going. We thought she was just scandalous. We had no idea what she was up to."

"So do you go to the fertility specialists one by one and see who cracks? I mean, they're not expecting that you're coming."

"That could take a long time," I said. There were ten clinics on the list and twice as many doctors.

"What would happen if I tried to get medical records on some of these places?" I asked.

"They'd claim privilege and by the time you went to court, the cat would be out of the bag," said Fiona.

"What does it take to do something like this?" I asked. "Put a baby in a girl that's not hers."

"The procedure is delicate, complicated and long," said Fiona. "And so whoever did it had help and access to expensive equipment as well as the DNA used."

I was thinking all manner of dark shit now. That the baby was being born for organs, to sell into slavery or it was Satan's.

Ivory had stuck her foot into something really bad, it cost the girl her life and now I was walking down the same dark path.

"Okay," I said. "The sooner I get going, the better then. Time to go knocking on doors the old fashioned way."

I gathered the information and left. I was going to see Bakersfield again and this time I didn't think it would be a pleasant meeting.

PART THREE: GRIND CITY

18

STAKES

Renardo was feeling low because he had failed. His goal was to become a better person, a better man but he had been pulled right back into the gutter, right back to violence.

White men. You just could not trust them. How could he have not seen that shit coming? He wanted to believe Thom was different but Renardo should have known better. None of them are different. They had no respect and really believed they were superior to other people.

He was going to get his money and then kill Thom and his ugly ass wife, he thought. He might even have to get rid of Kelvin. The man was weak and dumb, a bad combination in his line of work.

Thom might figure out he was marked and come prepared. But he could take him. Thom just thought he was a badass. He had no idea. Renardo had turned his mind and heart back to menace and he would not be stopped.

He was going to get out of the game, maybe move to Hawaii and chill on the beach. City life was stressful and he was not going to be one of those unfortunate black men in the graveyard.

He approached the home of Fred and Benetha Melvin, who owned the last house he needed on a city block. They were a nice, God-fearing couple who would not sell to him because of Reverend Payment.

But the reverend was gone now, having made his restitution and running scared of being exposed as a pervert.

The Melvins were the couple without vulnerabilities and that had presented a problem at first but Renardo was just gonna make them an offer over the value of the place then just split it with Thom. No need to get tough when you didn't have to.

He knocked on the door and Mrs. Melvin answered without opening.

"What is it you want, young man?" she asked.

"Just wanted to talk about the house again, maybe come to a deal," said Renardo.

The door opened and Mrs. Melvin stood with her husband, Fred. They look like an ad for a retirement home.

"Oh, it's you again," said Mr. Melvin.

"Yes," said Renardo. "Can I step inside?"

"Sure," said Mr. Melvin.

Renardo came in and was surprised to see Mr. Melvin putting aside a pistol.

"Sorry about the hardware," said Mr. Melvin. "Didn't know who it was. Been some trouble around here lately. Now, what about the house?"

"He wanted to talk about selling again," said Mrs. Melvin. "I didn't have a chance to tell him."

"Tell me what?" asked Renardo.

"The Reverend Paymer bought it from us last week," said Mr. Melvin. "Gave us a great price. Sorry."

Renardo's head grew light for a second. He did not believe that that charlatan would have the balls to do this. Forget about him and the gay hooker; he was going to kill that fat bastard.

"Oh, I didn't realize," said Renardo calmly. "Okay then, I'll just be going."

"You can stay and have some tea," said Mrs. Melvin. "It's real cold out there."

"No thank you, ma'am," said Renardo. "I have to get going but congratulations and good luck."

"Thank you young man," said Mr. Melvin.

Renardo walked back outside in the cold but he didn't feel it. He was raging inside. Payment would know he was coming and so he had to be cool about himself.

He got into his car and drove to Mount Holy Grace church on the west side of town. He got on his cell phone and called the good reverend. He had to wait for five minutes before the reverend got on the phone.

"Been waiting on your call, Mr. Peoples," said Reverend Paymer.

"You must really believe in God to be doing this," said Renardo. "I want my house back or I'll show you and the tranny to everybody."

"My wife filed divorce on me," said the Reverend. "So, I could give a shit. I don't want it to come out but it's not going to ruin me anymore. My congregation will understand. You can't tell what Impala has between her legs from that shot, so they will just think I had a girlfriend. My church will forgive me for that."

Renardo mumbled a curse and Paymer chuckled.

"Not so smart now, are you? See, I found out what that block is worth and you need that house. But it belongs to the church now. You want it back to complete that parcel, then give me that picture, my ten thousand and fifty-five more."

Renardo said nothing He wanted him to think that he was so pissed about it that he couldn't talk.

"I'll give you back the picture and the ten but that's it," said Renardo.

"You'll give me what I asked for you little punk or I'll screw up your deal with whoever wants that land. You gonna finance my lawyer fees for that woman I married."

"Fine," said Renardo, "but I need it now, today. I'm coming by in two hours."

"My deacons will be armed," said Paymer. "So, don't even think about trying me."

"Just have the quitclaim on you. I'll bring the contract."

Renardo hung up then cruised the neighborhood until he saw a young boy who had to be a drug dealer running between houses and cars.

Renardo stopped the boy and made a deal with him. He took the kid over to the church, set him up, then waited another hour before he moved in.

Renardo swung around the back of the place. It was empty. No one wanted to be outside in this cold and snow.

PART THREE: GRIND CITY

He took out his gun and waited by the back door. He could hear music inside, a choir rehearsal, he thought.

"Fuck with me," he muttered to himself breathing hard. He checked his watch and it was almost time.

Five minutes later, two loud shots rang out and the sound of shattering glass was heard as the young drug dealer fired into the church's front windows. There was screaming inside as the music stopped.

Suddenly, the door Renardo stood by flung open and Paymer and two big men ran out.

Renardo shot one of the men in the leg. He fell and screamed. The other he shot in the belly and he fell alongside the other one.

Renardo tripped Paymer and he fell flat on his face in the snow.

"Anybody moves and I'll kill you!" said Renardo.

He went to the deacons who were both yelling in pain and bleeding into the snow, removed their guns and threw them into a snow bank. He got Paymer to his feet and took him over to his car and had him open the door.

"Sign this deed and this contract or I will end you right here," said Renardo.

"You're crazy," said Paymer. "You can't shoot up a church."

"Sign it!" yelled Renardo and hit Paymer in the gut. He grunted as Renardo shoved a pen into his hand.

Paymer signed both documents. Renardo didn't care that it could be challenged. He just needed to show it to Thom. And it was the principle of it all. He would not let a stiff ass like Reverend Payment beat him at his game.

"You need to stay in your lane Rev," said Renardo. "You earned this."

Paymer yelled as Renardo shot him in the ass. The reverend grabbed himself and staggered away, blood running down his pants and into the white ground.

Renardo ran off as people started to come out of the front of the place. He would circle back to his ride and be gone before the cops or anyone else could come.

In the back of the church, the deacons yelled for help as Paymer clutched at his chest, gasping and fell on his side.

19

SERVICE

Dr. Bakersfield did not look happy to see me as I walked up to him in the hallway. He was doing rounds at Mercy Hospital. He looked busy and so I was catching him at good time for interrogation.

I was stone-faced as I waited for him to finish talking with some nurses and another doctor. When they all dispersed, he walked over to me.

"This can't be good if you're back, detective," said Bakersfield. "What is it?"

We walked over to an area where there were no people and I thought I saw his hand shaking.

"Ivory Shaw was pregnant," I said.

"What? It wasn't mine," he said. "We hadn't been together in months. No way."

"How do I know that? I'm gonna need some DNA, just to rule you out. You can fight it but then you'd need a lawyer and all kinds of questions might be asked— publicly."

"Jesus, Jesus," he said. "This is some kind of nightmare."

I knew it wasn't his baby but I needed him motivated.

"When Ivory stalked you, you said she came to your offices. How did she get in to see you?" I asked.

"She pretended to be a patient, said she needed a doctor, then she asked for a second opinion and like a fool, I walked in and there she was, half naked, grinning at me like the devil."

"Who was the other doctor?"

"One of my partners, Dr. Bell-Ross, Sandra."

"I'm going to need to talk to her," I said.

"She's not at the office," said Bakersfield. "She's been sick. Her husband called in for her."

I had a feeling of dread. I saw RaRa laying dead in Wyandotte and felt an urge to bolt for the door.

"When was the last time you saw her?"

"Three days ago, I think. She looked fine then."

I got Dr. Bell-Ross' number and address and then I had Bakersfield put some hair into an evidence bag and I left. I would make him sweat it out on the DNA test, or maybe I'd never call him back.

I called Dr. Ross on my way to her house but got her voicemail. I didn't leave a message and just kept driving out to Grosse Pointe Shores.

GPS was one of those areas that just made you mad when you went there. The homes were all huge with prices in the seven figures. I didn't know being a doctor was so lucrative. I guessed that Dr. Bell-Ross already had the money before she went to medical school.

Now it was making more sense to me. A rich person could throw a baby into an inner city girl and not be caught and who knows why rich people did the crazy shit they did these days.

PART THREE: GRIND CITY

The house on Lakeshore Road looked like something out of a travel brochure. It was enormous and the land seemed to go on forever. I was stopped by a guard who came out of a little booth.

"Detroit police," I said showing him my badge and ID. "Need to see Dr. Sandra Bell-Ross."

"The doctor's not well," said the guard who was a black man about sixty or so.

"She got a husband or grown kids I can talk to?" I asked. I was not buying this sick thing but I didn't want to piss the man off.

"Damn, I thought you was shittin' me with that voice," said the guard. "You a real wigger, huh?'

"We don't like the W-word," I said laughing. He laughed with me.

"I knew a white kid just like you," said the guard. "Donald Dees, a good man."

"Look, I know she ain't sick," I said. "I'm worried about her. When did you see her last?"

The guard looked around then moved closer to me.

"Something damned sure ain't right," he said. "The doc never came back home three days ago. Her husband's been around and he looks like shit. They ain't got no kids."

"Where was she coming from three nights ago, work?" I asked.

"Naw, she went to her yoga class. Got it on the schedule. She never came back. The day guard confirmed it. Husband's been acting like everything's okay, saying she's sick but none of the staff have seen her. You ask me, she's dead."

PART THREE: GRIND CITY

I got the husband's name, Thom Ross.

I got Dr. Ross' plate number and her husband's cell number from the guard but I was sworn to secrecy.

If I tried to question the husband, he would hide behind a gang of lawyers. If no one filed a missing persons on her, it could be a while.

If he had killed her, he would have made his move by now. The police would be out looking for her while her body was somewhere decomposing. He was still around the house and in the city, so that meant someone had snatched her. A kidnapping made more sense.

I said goodbye to the guard whose name was Horace and took the long drive back into the city. I could have waited for the husband but time was not on my side. Three days into a kidnapping was a long time. Chances were she'd be dead in a week if it went on that long. Otherwise, the husband would pay and everyone would pretend like it never happened. Either way, I'd never find my killer.

I went to the precinct and found the info on Dr. Bell-Ross' car. I knew a thief would ditch the plates but they could not change the vehicle ID. It was not on the stolen or found car list and so maybe it had been chopped up.

It was a high-end Mercedes AMG, so I took a chance that it had that service, Tele-Aid. It did and it was simple to get the tracking on it.

The service showed that the car left her yoga place at seven thirty-nine three days ago and then headed east. Then the signal went out.

PART THREE: GRIND CITY

I got the location and headed out. I had been running all day and it was already dark. I drove over the Detroit Grosse Pointe border and looked around but found nothing. If they ditched the ride, then someone took it and that was that. Smart move, I thought.

I was exhausted. Working alone was good but I wanted to have someone to bounce ideas off. I almost called Vinny but she'd want to come out with me and I didn't want that. The family was doing their thing and honestly, I didn't want her on the street this time.

I called Grosse Pointe PD but they had nothing on the car either. I decided to call it a night. I'd be refreshed the next day I told myself.

On my way back home, I called the Samoan again but again, I got no answer. His place was on the way back to my house, so I decided to drop by and get his favor out of my life.

The people living at Jimmy's were now all on the inside as it was much to cold to hang out in the old parking lot. The vans were still there though and I assumed business was going on inside them.

The inside of the place was an office but many of the walls had been knocked down and the debris cleared away. Graffiti covered the walls in vivid colors and on one wall, there was a full-sized portrait of Jimmy.

The people were still doing what they did, smoking drinking and partying. The fight pit was gone but many of the fighters were still there.

Jimmy and his crew were inside playing cards and dominoes and drinking. I saw Vollo at a table. When he saw me, the smile fell off his face.

"'Bout time," said Jimmy getting up.

"Been busy," I said. "What you need?"

"Nothing," said Jimmy. "I got something for you. Been calling for days now. Yo, that was some gangsta shit you did to that dirty cop."

Some of the crew echoed this statement.

"So, what can I do for you?" I asked impatiently.

"I need a rematch with you!" yelled Vollo. He had stood up and looked angry as hell.

"It's been a long day," I said. "Ain't got time to teach you another lesson."

The crew all laughed and Vollo pushed over a table and stormed over to me. Jimmy turned to him and stopped him with a look.

"You must wanna fight me," said Jimmy.

I took it that Jimmy was a good fighter because Vollo looked scared at these words. Jimmy was big and muscular and really quick on his feet. Didn't know if I could take him but Vollo knew and he took a step back.

"No," said Vollo.

"Go and get that new girl."

Vollo turned and walked out as Jimmy turned back to me.

"Excuse him," said Jimmy. "He's been upset since the fight. Boys been calling him Slap behind his back."

"Why am I here?" I asked.

"Got a new girl and she's trying to buy her way out of my service with information. She says her man kidnapped a rich white lady. Now, I'm thinking there's got to be a reward, right? I hook you up, you do the hero thing, then you help a brother out when you get her back."

Suddenly, I wasn't tired anymore. Some fool asses took Dr. Bell-Ross and one of them was bragging about it. If she wasn't dead, I just caught a break. Mentally, I was pissed because if I had gotten to Jimmy the first time he called, I could have been on this sooner, instead of chasing my ass around looking for that car, which was probably being sold in pieces all over metro Detroit by now.

"I'm listening," I said remaining cool.

Just then, my man Vollo walked in with a very pretty girl by his side. She walked over boldly and had no fear in her eyes.

"Yo woman, come over here," said Jimmy.

Vollo stopped and walked back to the crew while the girl came to us. She looked upset now that she was closer but that stood to reason as Jimmy was running his usual game on her. She glanced at me, then fixed her gaze on Jimmy.

"Who this?" said the woman.

"He can get you out of your situation," said Jimmy. "So, tell him what you told me, Impala."

20

TRACER

They still had no signal from her. Renardo had been smart. He'd ditched the car and her phone and purse but he had not taken her clothes and accessories, which was why Dr. Bell-Ross had a tracer in her earring.

The damned thing had to be damaged or something because it wasn't transmitting at regular intervals like it should have. They'd gotten a signal which led them in a general direction but it had gone out somewhere around mid-city.

Also, there was a lot of other crap signals in the air. With all the goddamned cell phones, drones and police activity it was a wonder the thing worked at all.

Thom Ross drove the Range Rover through the snowy streets looking for his wife. He had no intention of letting Renardo blackmail him. He had not wanted to resort to this but more death had to come now.

None of this had to happen but Sandra and her crazy family had pushed everyone to the extreme.

The family had a dynasty trust, which passed the family's legacy to each successive generation as soon as an heir was born. Of course, no one told him that when he was marrying the woman. He was never asked to sign a prenup and he thought he was getting away with something. He'd just stay married for a few years and then slam it on her, he'd thought.

Well, the family was protected because as soon as a kid was born, all of the money would go to that kid and he, Sandra and her brother and his wife would get just enough to live out their lives but no jackpot.

And if you divorced someone after an heir was born, well, you'd get part of what your spouse had, which legally was not much because the trust owned everything, the money, the cars, the real estate and investments, all of it.

Sandra even volunteered her services as a doctor, so he couldn't even get that money. He was fucked.

This was how rich people kept money in the family and kept gold-diggers from taking advantage.

He made sure not to get Sandra pregnant, even though she begged him for a kid.

Her brother Evan's wife could not have kids and that had frustrated him. And before he could dump her ass for a new wife, Evan, had had a ski accident and ended up a veggie. He died soon thereafter.

This devastated Sandra who had been very close to her brother all her life. They had survived cruel parents, boarding schools and more than a few personal tragedies.

But Sandra had tricked Thom and stole DNA to impregnate the black girl. She had done the procedure with some trusted friends but Thom found out and had to stop the kid from being born. He did but it had resulted with him being in league with even more dangerous people.

PART THREE: GRIND CITY

The man riding shotgun was silent as they drove around looking for a signal from Sandra's tracer. He held a little machine in his lap and occasionally raised it to the window to see if he could get better reception.

This was the man who had waited for Ivory Shaw in the precinct house and killed her. He'd sabotaged the surveillance system and had set up Dobbs Harson, who was the perfect, flawed patsy.

He killed Raymond Ranier after extracting information from him and he'd tracked down his mother but was too late that night.

When Dobbs Harson was arrested, he thought the whole thing was over. They'd all get the money, break the trust and cash out. But it got complicated because of Thom and this nigger he was in business with.

This had all been very hard on Officer Bill Wiznewski. As one of the original eight officers under suspicion, he had been very limited in what he could do in the aftermath. The IAD had been on him and he was getting pressure at home. He and his wife were calling it quits and the child support and alimony for their six kids would kill him. Women and kids were like death and taxes, he thought.

When Wiznewski's little half-sister Janet, the beauty queen, married into the Bell family, he was excited. Rich relatives were always a good thing. He and Janet were estranged back then and had not spoken in years. He wasn't even invited to the wedding.

Wiznewski had gone to her on his knees and they started talking again but as far as the Bells knew, he didn't exist.

PART THREE: GRIND CITY

But the Bell family was a bunch of assholes and had the money tied up and then the little shit of a brother in law died on them, but not before dropping the secret of what Sandra, his crazy, fucked up sister had been up to.

Wiznewski had been watching Dobbs Harson and the black girl meet for weeks after he knew she was carrying Sandra's heir. He'd followed her one night and saw her meet Dobbs at a crap motel. He could not believe it. Getting rid of her and that baby was going to be easier than he thought.

He needed a scapegoat and Dobbs was perfect. He was a loose canon and with all the police misconduct going on and the race-baiting in the media, he knew it would be a national story. He would even be suspected at first, then let go. It was all too perfect.

Suddenly, the little receiver beeped. A signal was coming in.

"Got something," said Wiznewski. "It's faint but it's got to be her."

"How far?" asked Thom.

"A good way, I think. Take Seven Mile at the next intersection. We're going in and take both of these guys out. And when this is over, we're all going to have to renegotiate things."

"Don't worry," said Thom. "They'll be plenty of money. We just need Sandra alive for now."

Wiznewski nodded but it was already planned that when it was all over, Dr. Sandra Bell-Ross was a dead woman.

21

REWARD

"What do you know about a kidnapping?" I asked the girl named Impala.

"This guy named Kelvin's been gettin' with me for a minute," said Impala. "He works with this other dude named Renardo. They run house scams on old people. Anyway, we been hookin' up here and there, not for long periods of time, you know, because his boss don't approve."

"Ask her why," said Jimmy excitedly.

I didn't ask, I just gave Impala a look.

"That's not important," she said. "We have to sneak to get it in. That's the only thing that's—"

"She got a dick!" said Jimmy. "Can you believe that? Look at that ass on her, them legs. Ain't a touch of man on her."

"I'm in transition," said Impala. "Like the universe."

I took another look and I almost didn't believe it. There was nothing masculine about the girl, not even her hands but I took Jimmy at his word. And yes, I was feeling a little uncomfortable because before Jimmy said this, I was digging her looks.

"Okay, so the boss don't approve, I said. And?"

"Well, Kelvin, he just wants me to go down on him and go real quick. So, I ask why and he tells me he got to get back because his boss done gone crazy. I didn't push for why. Always best to let a man take his time. Well, it didn't take long. Kelvin said Renardo got pissed because some rich white dude screwed him on a deal, so he took his wife."

"Was the woman a doctor?" I asked and I couldn't help that my voice rose a little in anticipation.

"Yeah, yeah," said Impala. "He said she was some big time doctor from rich people in GP."

"Where are they holding her?" I asked.

"This old building over by Mound Road," said Impala. "Kelvin said it used to be a canning plant or something."

I promised Jimmy a reward of there was one. I bolted out of there as soon as I could. If Dr. Bell-Ross was still alive, she probably didn't have long.

I got into my car and took the drive to case the place. I had to make sure this wasn't all bullshit before I called in the troops. The only plant in that area was the old Tulling Canning building.

As far as I could figure, Dr. Bell-Ross met Ivory while she was stalking Bakersfield and somehow talked her into being a surrogate, paying her off the books.

Ivory used her pregnancy to leverage her then boyfriend, Dobbs Harson. They fought and she went to see him at the precinct and was killed. So if Dobbs didn't do it, that meant one of the other cops was dirty. We missed something, some connection and it had cost us.

I arrived at the Tulling plant and staked it out. There was a car parked in the back of the place. From the front, it looked abandoned. This could definitely be it, I thought. I moved in closer on foot and managed to get a look inside.

I saw two black men sitting and watching a little TV. They each had guns on the table. They were having what looked to be a heated exchange.

There was a little back room. I assumed my victim was being kept there.

I pulled out my cell phone and called it in. I'd wait for the cavalry and hope they'd give up without a fight.

Suddenly, the two men started yelling at each other. This continued for a while and then one of them stood, grabbing a gun. I heard a noise, a car's engine revved loudly and then a Range Rover crashed through the front of the place.

****

"Don't believe you did that," said Kelvin. "A church, man."

"I was pissed off," said Renardo. "Man challenged me. What could I do?"

"Step off," said Kelvin. "You coulda stepped off. News say, that reverend had a heart attack and died. That's murder."

"Well, it be that way in the city. He knew the game. He had no business playing."

"Look, I ain't no religious man but—"

"Then shut the fuck up," said Renardo. "You ain't got no thing on me. You do shit, too."

PART THREE: GRIND CITY

"I'm just sayin' kidnapping and now murder. You fell off your promise. You back to what you used to be."

Renardo stopped playing the card game and looked at his friend. He was mad and that was just part of it.

"So what?" Renardo began. "Maybe this is who I am. My folks was decent, so I can't claim no hard life as a kid. I never went to the joint all the time I was slinging dope. Never got caught. I had plenty of time to get out but I didn't. I liked the life. I ain't got no boss, don't punch no clock and I get out what I put in. So if I put in kidnapping that bitch and murder, then maybe that's the price of a good life."

"Sorry but that don't make no sense," said Kelvin.

"What do you know about sense?" asked Renardo laughing. "You tried to hook up with a man."

"She ain't no man," said Kelvin.

"She got a dick, fool. Even if she gets it chopped off, it's still a man you fuckin.'"

"You prejudiced," said Kelvin.

"No, I'm a man," said Renardo. "I don't know what you are."

"I'm me and who I do it with ain't none of yo business." Kelvin looked away from his boss as he said this.

"Hold up," said Renardo noticing. "Did you… You been fucking around with that he/she, Impala?"

"None of yo business what I do off the clock, nigga."

"Everything you do is my business," said Renardo. "Did you suck his dick or did he fuck you in the ass with his lady cock?"

PART THREE: GRIND CITY

"Fuck off," said Kelvin. "At least I ain't going to hell for shooting a preacher."

"No, you goin' for sucking dick. Keep away from that thing. I don't want that on my rep. I don't roll with fags."

"I ain't no fag!" said Kelvin. He jumped up, grabbing his gun.

"Ain't this a bitch," said Renardo. "You better put that gun—"

A loud engine revved outside. In the instant, Renardo thought it must have creeped up with the lights off. A second later, a truck crashed through the boarded up front doors of the place.

****

I pulled both guns and kicked open the back door. As I waded in, I saw two men get out of the Range Rover. One of them was Bill Wiznewski, an original suspect. That answered that question. The other man, I didn't know.

The two men who had been arguing, had grabbed their guns and were raising them.

"Police!" I yelled without even thinking about it.

There was a second of confusion. In that instant, I fired the .45 at Wiznewski as he was the most dangerous. I hit him in the side and he fired his gun, missing me by a wide margin. He dropped the gun as he hit the ground.

PART THREE: GRIND CITY

I fired the Glock at the same time but it missed the two men who had been arguing. It didn't matter, because of one of them shot the other in the gut.

The man who had gotten out of the Range Rover with Wiznewski yelled "Fuck me!" then ran out of the building.

I'd swung to my right as the arguing man who'd shot his friend fired at me just as I shot at him.

His shot hit me and knocked me off my feet. I shot at him with both guns and hit him in the chest and head. Couldn't tell you which gun fired which shot.

Wiznewski got to his feet and moved back toward the Range Rover.

I hit the ground hard, the flack jacket I wore stopped the bullet but it hurt like shit. I got up and raised my guns, which I was shocked I had not dropped.

"Stop!" I managed to say to Wiznewski as I moved forward.

Wiznewski stopped moving. I moved over to him, while watching the other two fallen men. I kicked his gun away and removed the one I knew he was carrying in a leg holster. There was blood everywhere and Wiznewski was groaning.

"Move and I put one in your goddamned head," I said.

I went over to the other men. One was alive, the one I'd shot was gone. The dead man was dressed in a suit and tie. The one still alive just held his wound and cried.

"Call an ambulance!" said Kelvin, breathing hard. "I'm hit, man!"

"Where is she?" I demanded.

"In that room back there," said Kelvin breathing hard.

"She alive?"

"Yeah, I didn't have nothing to do with that. That was all on Renardo."

I collected their guns and waited. If I left, one of them might run off. The woman was still alive and she'd keep while the cops came.

I went to Wiznewski and put pressure on his wound. I didn't want to lose him. He had the most sorrowful look on his face I had ever seen.

"Big, bad Danny Cavanaugh," he said through his pain.

"Don't talk," I said.

"Do me a favor, put one right here in my head," said Wiznewski.

"Can't do that," I said. "Just hold on."

"All of this," said Wiznewski, "is God's Will."

The police came in minutes later. One of them had Thom Ross. He was crying saying, his wife had been kidnapped and he had tried to save her.

The paramedics stabilized Bill Wiznewski and the man named Kelvin. Renardo Peoples was dead.

Kelvin, who had not stopped confessing, kept saying that it was divine retribution, that Renardo had killed a reverend.

I had a fractured rib from the gunshot and the doc got me wrapped up good. I knew Vinny was going to be pissed, but I was okay and so I was glad for that.

PART THREE: GRIND CITY

We collected Dr. Sandra Bell-Ross who was just fine. She was hungry, cramped and smelled pretty bad but she was alive.

The husband was hugging her and confessing love but I wasn't buying it. He had rolled in with my killer and that meant he was involved. I had him arrested and he yelled all the way to the precinct.

I walked over to Dr. Bell-Ross whose hair was matted and makeup smudged on her face.

"Thank you, detective," she said.

"No problem, ma'am," I said. "I'm afraid your husband is not clean in this."

"Yes," she said. "None of us are."

22

DYNASTY

Kelvin Walker told his side of the story and was trying to get on TV. He blamed everything on his boss, who he said had forced him to take the doctor. With his criminal record, no one was buying it. He'd be doing at least ten years because even if he was telling the truth, he violated his probation and assisted in other crimes.

Jimmy got a reward from the Bell Family Trust and I was surprised when he offered to give me a cut. I declined and I told him to give it to Impala. I figured she needed it. Jimmy promised he would. I didn't really like Jimmy but he did have a code, and so I had a new contact on the street.

Delores Ranier was in rehab and doing well. She said she hated my father but he was the best sponsor she'd ever had.

Thom Ross was in police custody and would not be making bail as he was a flight risk. He denied it, but we knew he was working with Wiznewski.

Dr. Bell-Ross wasn't talking. She was now surrounded by an army of lawyers and had gone into hiding after paying Jimmy his reward. As far as we knew, she was not talking to her husband.

The prosecutor had made the connection to Wiznewski's half-sister but she was not talking either. If people had learned only one thing from watching cop shows, they knew they didn't have to talk.

Bill Wiznewski was the key to all of this. He was physically restrained and was under suicide watch, so there was a nurse and a police officer in his room and another officer in the hall.

His wife would not talk to him and we learned from her that they were about to get a divorce. Six kids on a cop's salary. That explained a lot.

Unlike the others, Wiznewski had refused to be represented by an attorney. The POA reps, Hunnington, Backus and many others had come to him and he spurned them all. "God is my counselor," was all he would say.

He did talk with Father Carrin from St. Joseph's and Bishop McCullen but neither one could persuade him to lawyer up.

Wiznewski's only statements were confessions to the murders. Other than that, he was silent and the police and the public felt that the secret, whatever it was, would go to the grave with him.

And then he did something no one saw coming, he asked to talk to me.

I went to see him as fast as I could. I wanted to know the story because we all needed some closure on this and I knew the system could let Thom Ross slip through if we weren't careful.

Wiznewski's face was that of a man lost to himself. It was like no one was in there. I was next to him by his

IV across from an officer who stood at attention by the window.

"The priests told me to do this," said Wiznewski.

"Father Carrin asked you to call me?" I asked.

"They didn't mention you by name, they just said tell your truth to someone you can trust. You're a cop and a Catholic. I see you drop your old man off at Mass sometimes."

I just nodded. I had shot and arrested Wiznewski and was ready to kill him if I had to. In a funny way, I could see his point.

"Then tell me why you killed them," I said.

"I did what God wanted me to," he said, "that's the thing."

He went silent on me and I could sense that he was having second thoughts. Whatever he was holding, was heavy. I decided to push a little.

"Why would you care about that kid?" I asked. "It was innocent and so was my sister in law."

"I did everything right!" said Wiznewski angrily.

The cop in the room turned to us and I waved him off.

"I served my country, two tours," Wiznewski continued. "I married my high school sweetheart. I was fruitful and we multiplied. I honored God and his laws and look what it got me. We barely make it in my house and then my wife decides after six kids that she wants to leave me for some guy because he makes a few more dollars. That guy's family left him and so he just takes mine. Money. That's all people care about."

I didn't say anything to get him back on track. I didn't want him to clam up on me. He obviously had some things on his mind.

"You may as well leave," said Wiznewski. "This was not a good idea."

"If you're thinking about your sister," I said, "this won't help her. We know she was married to Dr. Bell-Ross' brother. We'd never made the police connection because she doesn't use your last name. She's not talking but it's just a matter of time before Thom Ross breaks and throws you all under the bus. The prosecutor will cut a deal with the first person who does. You know the drill."

Wiznewski sat up sharply in bed. "Janet had nothing to do with this," he said.

"I can believe that," I said. "But I'm not the prosecutor."

Wiznewski took in a deep breath and thought a moment. He didn't have any leverage. Jesse King had released the other cops, except Dobbs Harson. Jamilla Cole was even reinstated quietly, pending lesser charges.

"I want to talk to my sister," he said.

Since Wiznewski was not represented by a lawyer, I arranged the call. I watched as tears welled in his eyes while he listened to his sister confirm what I had just told him. He said goodbye and handed me back my phone.

He just sat there for a while and I felt like he wanted to check out if he could. I was beginning to think it was all over, when he spoke:

"The trust," said Wiznewski. "That damned trust cut out my sister when Evan Bell died. Then it was going to cut out Thom Ross if Dr. Ross had a baby. But Thom and Dr. Ross both had reproductive problems and Thom didn't want the damned baby. He wanted the money. My sister couldn't get pregnant. Goddamned ovaries were busted up, probably happened when she was a teenager. She was in a bad car accident."

"Why didn't Dr. Ross just adopt?" I asked

"The baby had to be natural," said Wiznewski. "Blue blood, rich people shit."

"Then whose baby is it?" I asked. "We know it's not Dobbs Harson's or Ivory's. Is Thom Ross the father?"

"You ain't nearly as smart as people say," Wiznewski laughed darkly. "Don't you see it? It was Sandra and her brother Evan's baby."

I almost told him to stop fucking with me but his face was as serious as anything I'd ever seen. He was not lying.

This is why Dr. Bell-Ross was not talking. She had probably pumped herself with fertility drugs, then fertilized her own egg with her brother's sperm after his death and implanted it in Ivory. I bet that when we checked, we'd find that Evan Bell had sperm frozen when trying to get his wife pregnant.

In Dr. Bell-Ross' mind, the baby her husband would not give her and the one her brother would never have would be born and inherit the dynasty trust and she would forever be bonded to Evan.

PART THREE: GRIND CITY

No legit doctor would do this and so Dr. Ross had done it herself, probably with the help of another physician or two who she paid handsomely.

"Evan and Dr. Ross were close growing up, so close people thought it was creepy," said Wiznewski. "The father beat the hell out of them and the mother looked the other way and that bonded them."

"Were they sleeping together?" I asked.

"Who knows," said Wiznewski, "but it was as close as you could get the way I hear it. When Sandra married someone from the other side of the tracks, so did Evan. See what I mean?"

"How did Thom Ross know it wasn't his baby?"

"He thought it was at first. Dr. Ross lied to him, saying she had drugged him and stolen his sperm. See, she planned to pass it off as his kid in the end, but when Evan died, he confessed to my sister on his deathbed, then she told me and Thom."

"So Thom Ross agreed to give you and your sister money if you got rid of the baby," I said.

"He was already giving me money now and then to help. But the trust money would solve all of our problems. But Janet didn't know any of this. This was all between me and Thom."

"So Thom had you get rid of the heir and then you'd kill his wife after you somehow broke that trust," I said. I was not asking. This had to be the end game.

"Yes," said Wiznewski. "I was a cop and a soldier. Killing would come easy for me, the way he saw it. He was wrong about that."

"Didn't Dr. Ross catch on when Ivory was killed?" I asked. I was trying to see if Dr. Ross was somehow involved in the cover up.

"She might have been suspicious," said Wiznewski. "But Thom was still acting like it was their baby and then she thought Dobbs Harson did it like everyone else. And me? That woman doesn't even know I exist. Anyway, what was she going to do? Tell the police it was her incest baby?"

"And so, I guess it was you who disabled the cameras at the 11th that night," I said.

"I saw the girl's car pass the station," he began. "I'd been following her and so I knew who she was. I disabled the surveillance system at the junction box. That also disabled the cell door where I put her. She met Dobbs near that rear cell in a bathroom. They argued. Dobbs walked out. When she came out, I grabbed her… She fought, but I kept telling myself she was carrying an abomination in her belly."

Wiznewski's face had an almost insane look on it now as he relived it. I was numb. I had seen some pretty dark things in my career, but this took them all.

"That girl," said Wiznewski, "I didn't kill much. She was no good, a little whore, a sinner."

Before I could think, my hand shot out and grabbed his throat and squeezed. Wiznewski didn't fight me. I saw eagerness in his eyes.

The officer in the room took a step towards me, his hand on his sidearm.

"Sir, you have to let him go!" he said urgently.

I released him and backed away from the bed.

PART THREE: GRIND CITY

"Sorry," I said. "I just…"

"Go on," said Wiznewski still choking a little. "Finish it. No one will blame you."

The cop moved next to Wiznewski just to let me know there would be no more mistakes.

"The girl you killed had nine brothers and sisters," I said, pointing a finger at Wiznewski. "That's four more kids than you have. Her parents raised them all while being poor and black and they never had to do the evil shit you did to survive. I don't wish death on any of your kids as retribution because you've already killed your family, you just can't see it yet."

Wiznewski said nothing. He slumped in the bed and started to sob.

"You should leave now," said the nurse who had been watching all of the drama. "And you may want to see a doctor before you go. You don't look so good, officer."

I left the hospital and when I stepped outside, the cold air refreshed me as it tingled my face and body. It was like I was waking up from a nightmare. I stood there for a moment, just breathing and then I headed to my car.

I went over to the prosecutor's office to tell them what I knew. Thom Ross had already broken by now and confessed all of it implicating Wiznewski and his sister but he had not told the dark story of test tube incest.

Jesse King was floored by my story and looked visibly shaken. He was bringing cases against Kelvin

Walker, Thom Ross, Wiznewski and his sister, Janet Bell. It was going to be a grand slam for him.

Dr. Ross was the exception. She had not committed any crime, really, but she would have to close her practice when the news came out. She'd probably just disappear into her fortune and move out of the country. The rich people never go to prison, I thought. Never.

I stood for a moment, looking at the frozen city and I felt a sense of calm wash over me. Justice was going to be done and that was always good but there was something else, a sense of renewal that encouraged me. Suddenly, the city didn't seem so bad or nearly as cold as before.

PART THREE: GRIND CITY

Epilogue

Walking

The Shaw family was going to get a big settlement from the city. Marshall was orchestrating it. The kids all agreed that their parents should get the money. They'd do the right thing with it. It didn't feel right somehow, but this was all they had.

The Black Lives Matter people moved on to the next city. Hard to believe police shootings are now an industry.

DeAngela Gomez was now a full-fledged celebrity. She had been on four national news shows and had even landed in a New York paper in a best dressed column.

She and James Cole had broken it off and she was back on the prowl but had plenty of suitors. Knowing her, she was looking for a wealthy man to back her ever-expanding ambitions.

DeAngela and the IAD brass had even offered me a job. I imagined me and her as the poster kids for law and order and then I imagined Vinny shooting us both.

I turned them down of course, but I have to say, I was a little flattered.

I took some well-deserved time off. I stayed at home, played with the baby and acted like a normal human being. Children, I thought, to some a blessing, to others, a curse.

I discovered that I have an online presence now because some kids have started websites and Twitter accounts with my name on them.

There's one guy who goes by the name Danny Cavanaugh357 and he tweets tough guy talk in a reprehensible black slang. I would really like to find him and have a little talk about respect.

There are memes of me firing two guns and one of me half-naked. It's my face but I have no idea whose body that is.

Vinny tells me I can have them all pulled down if I wanted but that would only give them more attention. I figure after a while, they'll all disappear.

After a week, I had to sit down with a reporter and give him that interview. The story came out a week later and generally, I hated it. The word "hero" was used liberally. But I did get to say something important to me. I said, no matter what, we, the police, are still the good guys.

There is another part of the article I like and it sums up how I felt about everything. What it says about me, I'll let others decide.

Detroit Free Press:

DARK, BIZARRE TURNS IN
PRECINCT MURDER CASE

… Ivory Shaw and Raymond Ranier's killer knew that our current problems

in law enforcement would hide his
devious crimes. He knew that all of us
would go straight to past atrocities
and find comfortable enemies and
convenient racial positions which
would have us so angry and preoccupied
with our own self-righteousness that
we'd never suspect anything more evil
than our own hearts. Which brings me
back to Detective Cavanaugh, a man
who stands taller than his occupation
but tries to shrug off this shine because
he is embarrassed by it. His heart is not
evil and so he suspected everyone.
Thank God he did.

I'm going to save that for my son and one day when
he thinks his old man is corny and out of touch, I'll give
it to him. Then again, I had to have my own son to see
how cool my dad was, didn't I?

Vinny and me never talked about the fact that I got
shot and had I not been wearing a vest, I might have
bought it. No one wants to think about death around
our house these days.

RMC got up and walked a few days ago. He was
wobbly and he fell but he got right back up and came
to his mother.

I was happy of course but I had a flash of Bill
Wiznewski, whose kids had bound him in desperation
and Dr. Ross, whose desire for a child bound her to the

corruption of her very soul. My son was life and I was thankful for it.

The thought passed quickly as I envisioned RMC walking and running in the sun, a whole new world for him under his own power.

And so I turned to thoughts beyond the thick winter outside, to the renewal of spring, which would bring back life and hope.

GARY HARDWICK

THE AMERICAN GAME

A Luther Green Mission
BY THE AUTHOR OF *THE EXECUTIONER'S GAME*

Luther Green has survived the Executioner's Game and gone back to work eliminating threats to America around the globe.

When a trusted friend asks for his assistance in finding a government asset who faked his death on September 11th, Luther is drawn into another lethal game of cat and mouse, only this time, the fate of American hangs in the balance.

The government asset has proof of what happened that fateful day and how it was just the beginning of something even more sinister and deadly.

Luther sets out to undo the plot but when he is targeted by powerful forces, he is left no choice but to use all of his training to eliminate them all.

Praise For *The Executioner's Game*

"Far from being a shoot-'em-up, reaches into the psychological and emotional life of the hero, giving insight into the double-timing, dangerous and distrusting world of undercover work." -BIBR

"This exciting espionage thriller grips the audience from start to finish as if a non-stop heavyweight championship with the loser probably counted out for life." - Mystery Gazette

On Sale September 11, 2016